MOONLIGHT WARRIORS

A Tale of Two Hit Men

Joseph P. Rogers

iUniverse, Inc.
New York Bloomington

Moonlight Warriors

A Tale of Two Hit Men

Copyright © 2008 by Joseph P. Rogers

iUniverse books may be ordered through booksellers or by contacting:

iUniverse
1663 Liberty Drive
Bloomington, IN 47403
www.iuniverse.com
1-800-Authors (1-800-288-4677)

ISBN: 978-0-595-53126-4 (pbk)
ISBN: 978-0-595-51879-1 (cloth)
ISBN: 978-0-595-63188-9 (ebk)

Printed in the United States of America

iUniverse rev. date: 11/20/08

Praise him, sun and moon, praise him, all you shining stars.

Psalm 148:3

Sun and moon stood still in the heavens at the glint of your flying arrows, at the lightning of your flashing spear.

Habakkuk 3:11

The sun has one kind of splendor, the moon another, and the stars another; and star differs from star in splendor.

1st Corinthians 15:41

CHAPTER I

▼

THE ASSASSIN STRIKES

In the conference rooms of a hotel in New York City, a biotechnology conference neared the conclusion of the afternoon's scheduled activities. Biotechnology companies presented their latest products in order to persuade potential investors to purchase stock in their companies.

In the hotel's auditorium, Douglas Neldt addressed a crowded room. "Recent advances in technology have made it possible for us to develop this wonderful artificial intelligence program. Our team of programmers has been working on this biotechnology software for almost three years. When we demonstrate our Intelligent Agency program tomorrow morning, I guarantee that you will be amazed. The program can create a perfect three-dimensional replication of every virus that exists or has ever existed. It can then show the best way to destroy that virus. The Intelligent Agency program will save millions of lives every year."

A murmur went through the crowd upon hearing such a grandiose claim. One man in the upper balcony of the auditorium, though, was barely listening to the speech. From where he had been standing at the back of the room, he moved inconspicuously into a projection room that was not being used that afternoon.

He set his briefcase on the shelf next to the video projector, opened the case, and began to snap together the parts of his rifle. Working with a calm efficiency, he quickly assembled the rifle. Each rifle part made a decisive clicking sound that assured him that the part was firmly in place.

The man in the dark projection room rested his elbow on the ledge as he looked through the scope and took careful aim with the rifle. He focused the crosshairs on Neldt's forehead. The man only planned to take one shot and wanted to be certain that shot would be fatal.

Meanwhile, Neldt continued with his speech. "This program will provide our nation with a great defense against biological weapons. In this age of terrorism, this is especially important. If the terrorists attack us with a doomsday virus, Intelligent Agency can provide a cure. If the terrorists attack us with antibiotic-resistant bacteria, Intelligent Agency can design a drug that will kill the bacteria.

"The artificial intelligence of this program is truly amazing. The program has the capability to improve itself; if it's presented with some viral agent that it doesn't recognize, the program will adapt itself so that it's able to understand this new virus and determine the best way to destroy it. Intelligent Agency will probably grow in ways that we have not imagined. I'm certain that we can expect some surprises."

Hearing this last comment, the man paused before firing. He grinned slightly. Here is your first surprise, he thought as he squeezed the trigger.

The gunshot resounded through the auditorium. Douglas Neldt fell straight back as the bullet penetrated the center of his forehead. As he toppled backwards, Neldt knocked over the American flag behind the podium.

Pandemonium erupted, and the assassin used the chaos to his advantage. He slipped out the projection room's back door. Once in the hallway he easily merged in with the crowd fleeing from the auditorium, and he successfully escaped from the scene of his crime.

David Hummel and Sam Troutman arrived at the scene of the shooting less than fifteen minutes after the assassination occurred.

The two FBI agents were a study in contrast. David was only five foot five inches tall while Sam, being six foot three inches tall, towered over his partner.

David felt that Sam looked down upon him in more ways than one. David had never traveled outside of the United States; Sam had traveled throughout the world and was considered one of the FBI's experts on the Middle East and Europe.

Although he was not a world traveler, within his active mind, David had journeyed along many fascinating roads. He was fairly certain that he was the only FBI agent with a bachelor's degree in astronomy.

Astronomy was proving to be a lifelong hobby rather than a vocation; for various reasons, after receiving his astronomy degree, he had gone on to Notre Dame Law School and then joined the FBI after graduating.

David was also a chess champion; he had won several regional tournaments and was constantly trying to improve his game by reading chess strategy books.

As they stood in the lobby of the hotel, the cell phones of the two FBI agents rang almost simultaneously. The ringtones of the two phones harmonized smoothly, causing both men to laugh.

Their smiles soon disappeared, though, upon hearing the news from their callers. A few minutes ago there had been a series of explosions in the offices of Douglas Neldt's biotechnology software company. The offices had been almost completely destroyed and most of the employees had been killed by the explosions and subsequent fires.

"This definitely seems to be the work of terrorists," David said. "They must to be trying to put an end to that anti-viral computer program."

"It seems likely that all copies of the program have vanished in blood and fire," Sam said.

"Blood and fire," David echoed.

After speaking to many persons who had been in the auditorium, David and Sam selected Rebecca Wright as the person who could provide the most illumination on the case. Rebecca, a computer programmer at Neldt's company, was a tall, red-headed young woman.

They led Rebecca away from the television cameras and aggressive reporters.

"I like to think that the FBI helps to bring order out of chaos," David said as they walked out of the crowded hallway. "It should be more peaceful up there." They went up to the skywalk that extended over the street between the convention center and the hotel.

Along the skywalk's glass walls were some cushioned benches. Rebecca and the two men sat down on one of these benches.

"Oh, it's good to be able to relax for awhile!" Rebecca declared with a sigh. "I can't believe this is really happening."

"Did you know Douglas Neldt well?" Sam asked.

"Not especially well. Two years ago he recruited me for his company while I was doing graduate work in computer simulations of viruses and bacteria. He would occasionally meet with our programming team. He was always nice and polite, but he wasn't much for chit-chat with employees."

"I see," Sam said.

"We are working on the assumption that terrorists are responsible for the assassination and the bombing at your company," David said. "I hope that your company has some backup copies of that anti-viral computer program stored off-site somewhere. It would certainly be tragic if the terrorists succeeded today."

"Yes, it would be tragic. The project has been seriously damaged, but we should be able to continue our work. It will take us a few months, though, to get back to the point where we were before today's events." She raised her laptop computer so that the men could see it better. "I have a lot of the key files on this computer. My laptop computer, of course, isn't powerful enough to run the full version of the Intelligent Agency biotechnology software. However, there's a company in St. Louis that also has an almost complete comprehensive backup copy of our Intelligent Agency program."

"What company?" David inquired, somewhat surprised.

"Sandhaven Software Solutions."

The two agents spoke with Rebecca for several more minutes, then after verifying her contact information, told her that she could go home.

After she departed, David studied his notes, contemplating what they had learned since arriving at the hotel. Sam, who was by nature more reticent than David, also remained silent, absorbed in his own thoughts.

David finally broke the silence. "I don't understand why the assassin shot Douglas Neldt here in front of an audience. The assassin could have killed him somewhere else with much less risk of being captured. Douglas Neldt did not have a bodyguard; he was not a famous person."

"Perhaps he would have been famous someday if his Intelligent Agency program lived up to its glory," Sam interjected.

David continued to flip through his pages of notes. "But the assassin could have shot him at the supermarket or in front of his home. Anywhere but here would have been so much simpler."

"I guess that we'll have to catch the assassin so that we can ask him," Sam said, then added with a hint of disdain in his voice, "You're not going to find your answers in those papers."

"You never know," David replied with a rueful grin. He knew that Sam, who considered himself a man of action, considered David to be a bookworm and was not impressed by David's scholarly approach to their work.

Then, as if some sudden epiphany had occurred, David looked up from the papers, his eyes wide. "The assassination was carried out in a dramatic manner in order to send a message."

"What message?"

"Don't continue this project. Don't attempt to restart the project."

"You might be correct about that," Sam acknowledged. "In fact, I can't think of any other explanation. And blowing up Neldt's company certainly reinforced that message."

"Right."

They headed back toward the projection booth in the auditorium in order to search for any clues that might have been overlooked.

At dusk the next day, Rebecca Wright disembarked from the commuter train and walked onto a tree-lined street of the quiet suburb. I might miss all the oak trees and lovely scenery if I move downtown, she debated with herself.

Her apartment building was located about a quarter-mile from the train station. Rebecca glanced over her shoulder occasionally as she walked at a somewhat brisker pace than usual. All day she had felt like she was being watched, although she had not actually seen anyone following her.

Rebecca carried a briefcase containing her laptop computer. Until a few months ago she had used a padded leather carrying case for transporting the computer, but she decided that the carrying case made it too obvious to potential thieves that an expensive computer was inside. Therefore, she purchased a briefcase in order to give the appearance that she was only carrying papers.

Rebecca walked past the tennis courts and up one flight of steps onto the walkway that led to her apartment. Once again she looked back to make certain that no one was following her.

She unlocked her apartment door, stepped inside, and shut the door behind her. As soon as Rebecca flicked on the light switch, she was grabbed from behind.

A hand tightly clasped over her mouth made it impossible for her to shout for help. Rebecca tried to hit the attacker with her briefcase, but he was behind her, making it difficult for her to reach him.

Then she felt a knife enter her back and pierce her heart. She collapsed dead to the floor, never having seen the face of her murderer.

The man removed the knife from his victim, used a tablecloth to wipe the blood off the blade, and placed the knife back in the sheath in his jacket.

After picking up the briefcase, he placed it on the table and snapped it open. He took out the laptop computer.

The man then completed his search of the apartment, a search that he had begun before Rebecca had returned home. About five minutes after the murder, the man departed from the apartment, taking with him some of her papers and her computer.

CHAPTER 2

▼

LOVE WILL LEAD US HOME

"**Love will lead us home.**" -- This message was emblazoned in gold letters on the blue tee-shirts worn by a group of teenagers that walked past Marcus on the sidewalk.

Marcus Augustine was not a man who was easily distracted. Even though he was in the middle of a mission, Marcus paused for a few moments as he read the message on the high school students' shirts.

The picture on the shirts depicted three travelers on horseback, perhaps they were knights, as they rode toward a holy city illuminated by a glowing cross.

It reminded Marcus of a purer, truer, better time of his life. For those few moments, it reawakened and renewed all of his hopes.

Chance and circumstance had conspired against him.

Marcus Augustine realized at a young age that he was not going to be one of those fortunate few who seemed to coast through life with ease.

When he was ten years old, his parents were driving to a funeral of a family friend when a truck driver smashed into the rear of their car, killing both his mother and father. In order to make a few extra dollars, the truck driver had stayed on the road too long without sleep and had not noticed that the traffic ahead of him had come to a stop.

His greed killed my parents, Marcus reflected bitterly. He killed them in a funeral procession. Marcus realized the cruel irony of the tragedy. The funeral procession for his parents traveled down the same road a couple of days later.

Marcus was an only child. He had been in school on the day of the accident, so his life was spared.

He went to live with his aunt and uncle, who were pleasant persons, but they were no comparison to his own parents. They had four children of their own and his presence made their small house even more crowded.

Marcus lived with this family for eight years; there were no major problems, but he always felt like an outsider intruding upon them. He was never completely comfortable there.

A few days after his eighteenth birthday, Marcus signed up for the Army. He was glad to finally be out of that house. He suspected that his aunt, uncle, and cousins were relieved to see him go, but they expressed regret at his departure.

Soon after bidding them farewell, he was on a bus to the military base where he would receive basic training. Somewhat to his own surprise, he did exceptionally well during basic training. He was smart, a good athlete, tough, and self-disciplined.

Marcus realized that he was the best recruit at the camp. During training drills, the others seemed almost to be moving in slow motion compared to him.

The officers quickly realized that he was special forces material, and Marcus was transferred to another base where he received this special forces training.

He excelled there, completed his training, and was sent with his unit to Afghanistan where they carried out top-secret, anti-terrorist operations.

Marcus loved the military, and he was awarded for his outstanding service. He was happy there. Eventually, though, he became frustrated by all the rules and regulations. The rules of engagement were too strict, too inflexible. Many of their jihadist enemies were operating out of bases in nearby countries, but they were not allowed to attack them in those countries.

Marcus wanted to kill the evildoers no matter where they were, and he wanted to use any means necessary to accomplish his mission.

After leaving the military, Marcus moved back to the St. Louis area where he established himself as a private detective. He had intended to work as an ordinary private investigator. However, after seeing women and children being abused, he decided to deal with the cowardly bullies in the way that he had been trained to do. With help from Marcus, several men, who would be missed by no one, disappeared from the face of the earth.

His thoughts returned to the present. Marcus realized that he had lost sight of the two men whom he had been following. Setting aside his reflections, he hurried forward, scanning the pedestrians ahead of him on the busy downtown street.

He soon spotted the two young men; they were only a half-block ahead of him. They turned onto a side street and went into a bakery.

Marcus approached the small store and then stopped outside the open doorway. He leaned casually against the brick wall and listened to the conversation taking place within.

"We need that money today!" declared one of the men.

"Today's cash has already been deposited in the bank," explained an older woman. She and her husband were the co-owners of the bakery.

"You owe us two thousand dollars for our protective services," the other man told her. "You need our protection. Bad things happen to good people."

"Then you two don't have to worry about something bad happening to you," the husband said as he came out of the back room and approached the counter.

"Hey, old man, don't disrespect me!"

"Respect has to be earned."

The first young man looked at the husband intently. "We might teach you to respect us by burning this bakery to the ground."

"Yeah," laughed the other man. "Lew's Laundry over on the next block burned down last week. We taught him to respect us."

"You think so?" the wife said, shaking her head in disdain.

"I don't like the attitude that you two have!" the first man shouted at them. "You need an attitude adjustment!"

The second man approached the couple menacingly. "Unless you give us that two thousand dollars now, you are going to be hurt bad." He grabbed the older man's shirt and pulled the owner toward him.

This situation is starting to get out of control, Marcus thought. I'd better intervene now. He stepped through the doorway.

All four persons inside glanced toward him.

"Good afternoon," Marcus said, taking several steps forward. "I would like to purchase a half-dozen doughnuts."

"Come back later," the first man said.

"I'm going to need those doughnuts now. My schedule is very busy today."

"The bakery is closed for the day," the second man told Marcus. "There was a death in the family."

"And there might soon be another one," the first man chuckled.

Marcus ignored them and approached the counter where a wide variety of cakes, cookies, doughnuts, and other pastries were on display.

"Everything looks so good," Marcus said. "I think that I'll get a Danish roll along with the doughnuts."

"Are you deaf?" the second man shouted at him. "This place is closed!"

"It looks open to me."

"If you don't leave right now, I'm going to hurt you bad." The man moved toward Marcus, intending to grab him.

Instead, Marcus grabbed the man's arm and broke his wrist. As the man screamed in pain, his partner flipped open a butterfly knife and lunged at Marcus.

Marcus deftly avoided the blade, kicked the man in the groin, and hit him in the head with a backfist strike. He restrained the dazed man, took away his knife, and removed the handgun from the man's jacket.

Marcus shoved both men out the doorway. They stumbled onto the sidewalk, and after a few seconds, went staggering away, muttering curses and threats.

The bakery owners looked at Marcus with amazement.

"Thank you!" the husband said.

"Who are you?" the wife asked.

"A couple of days ago, I was hired by your neighborhood association to protect your businesses from the gang that has been terrorizing them."

"Oh!" the husband explained. A look of understanding appeared on his face. "Yes. We contributed to the fund that was raised to pay your fee. That gang has killed four persons in this neighborhood. They even murdered a teenage girl to keep her from testifying against them. Last week they burned down Lew's Laundry, and Lew was badly burned trying to save his business. We realized that extreme action needed to be taken."

"Yes. You did the right thing to hire me. I will take care of the problem."

"But those gangsters will be back!" The wife declared with wide eyes. "They will be furious about what happened to them in our store. Next time they will kill us!"

Marcus moved toward the doorway. "You will never be bothered by those two men again. And soon the rest of the gang will no longer be a problem."

"You are one man," the wife said. "Can you defeat an entire gang?"

"I guess that we will find out soon enough," Marcus said with a smile.

"Go do what needs to be done," the husband said. "Good luck, and God bless you."

Marcus went out the door and headed down the street in the direction that the two men had gone. He hoped that he could catch them.

After walking for about a block, he still did not see them. He began to worry that they had called someone to pick them up.

I lingered in that store too long talking to that couple, Marcus reprimanded himself. I allowed those guys to get too much of a lead on me.

Then, a half-block ahead, he spotted them walking into an alley where a third man was waiting for them. After conferring briefly with this third man, all three pulled out their cell phones and made calls.

Bingo! Marcus thought as he advanced toward the men.

They were so intent with their phone conversations that they did not notice Marcus until he was about thirty feet from them.

The man with the broken wrist dropped his cell phone and reached into his jacket and began to pull out a handgun.

With the swiftness of a classic western gunfighter, Marcus did a quick draw of his own pistol from the shoulder holster concealed beneath his leather jacket.

As the man started to aim the gun at him, Marcus fired a silenced shot through his forehead. He fell dead onto the hard pavement of the alley.

The third man, who had his own gun pulled halfway out of his pocket, froze as Marcus aimed at him.

"That would be a really bad idea," Marcus warned. "Drop the gun and kick it toward me."

The man did so, and Marcus picked up the gun and placed it into an inner pocket of his jacket.

"You killed Scott!" the second man shouted accusingly at Marcus.

"He didn't give me much choice, did he?" Marcus said. "I hope that the two of you make smarter choices than your friend did."

"What do you want?" the third man asked.

"At the moment I want your wallets and your cell phones. And give me the wallet and cell phone of your dead friend." When they hesitated, Marcus aimed his gun at them. "You know that I will pull the trigger. Give me those wallets and cell phones now!"

Realizing that he was not bluffing, the two men quickly complied, handing Marcus their wallets and cell phones. The third man removed Scott's wallet from the back pocket of his jeans, picked up the cell phone from the alley pavement, and handed both item to Marcus.

"I can't believe this!" the second man exclaimed. "You are robbing us!"

"No, I'm not." Keeping one eye on the men, Marcus removed the driver's licenses and some other identification cards from the wallets, then tossed all three wallets back to them. "I didn't take any of your money or any credit cards. I just want to know who the three of you are and where you live. I want the cell phones because I'm going to use their call logs to help identify the other members of your gang."

"Who are you?" the third man asked.

Marcus could tell that this man was the smartest of the three. "I am a concerned citizen."

"Come on, man."

"I am concerned that your gang has been terrorizing this neighborhood. Your gang has killed four persons in this neighborhood, including a teenage girl who was going to testify against you. Last week you burned down a laundry and the owner was badly burned. Justice would be served if I killed both of right here, right now."

"We didn't do anything, man," the second man insisted.

"I want the names and addresses of the leaders of your gang. I want the names and addresses of whoever killed the teenage girl."

"What are you going to do to them?" the third man asked.

"What do you think?" Marcus replied.

"We're not telling you anything, man," the second man said.

"I can see some gentle persuasion is going to be necessary." Marcus aimed his gun downward and fired a silenced shot that ricocheted off the pavement only inches away from the second man's foot.

"Hey!" The man jumped back in fear. "Why did you do that?"

"Unless you two tell me who killed that teenage girl, I'm going to have to assume that you two are the killers. Or you might be leaders of the gang. Then I will be the judge, jury, and executioner."

The third man glanced down at Scott's body. "Neither of us had anything to do with murdering the girl, and we are not leaders."

Keeping his gun trained on them, he handed a pen and paper to the third man.

"Tear that piece of paper in half, and give him the other half," Marcus commanded. "I want each of you to write down the names that I want. Don't look at each other lists."

A couple of minutes later both men completed the assignment that Marcus had given them. He briefly examined the two lists.

"Fortunately for both of you, these two lists agree," Marcus said. "You gave me the same names. There are a couple of minor differences in addresses and phone numbers, but I should be able to resolve that problem." Marcus paused and looked closely at the two men. "I'm going to allow both of you to live --- at least for now. However, you must not do anything else to harm or threaten anyone in this neighborhood. And you must not tell anyone about the information that you gave me."

"There's not much chance of us telling anyone," the second man said. "We don't want to be called snitches."

"You've done the right thing," Marcus said as he began walking toward the street. "You both can still turn your lives around and get on the right path."

The third man glanced down at Scott's body. "Here is a dead man. You killed this man. What makes you think that you are on the right path?"

Marcus returned his pistol to its holster. "I'm not on the right path yet, but I'm searching for it. Good luck."

The two men watched as Marcus departed from the alley and turned the corner onto the street, vanishing from their view.

In the following week, Marcus completed his mission. The three cell phones had proved to be gold mines of information.

The numerous voice mail messages to which he gained access provided him with many valuable insights into the gang and its activities.

Marcus tracked down, set up, and eliminated the three key leaders of the gang. After doing a short investigation, Marcus conclusively determined that one of those leaders had personally murdered the teenage girl who had planned to testify against the gang.

Marcus did not enjoy killing, but he had to admit to himself a certain amount of personal satisfaction at delivering justice to this man who had murdered the young woman. That gang leader thought that he had escaped the justice system by murdering her, Marcus reflected. However, justice caught up with him anyway, and he got what he richly deserved --- a bullet in the head.

Marcus was glad that he did not need to kill any of the lower-level gang members. Marcus correctly reasoned that the gang would fall apart without any leadership.

As soon as he was certain that his mission was complete, Marcus logged onto the Internet and used a travel website to book a Caribbean vacation. He left his own cell phone back at his expensive condo in Clayton. Marcus wanted and needed two weeks of complete relaxation --- sailing, snorkeling, sand, and sun.

CHAPTER 3

▼

JENNY JAWBREAKER

It was a little, neighborhood diner with a big reputation. Angie's Place was noted for its first-rate hamburgers, seafood, and several types of soup.

The diner was located in southeast St. Louis about a quarter-mile from a popular Mississippi River casino. In addition to its good food, Angie's Place had a reputation for being a meeting place for persons engaged in various illegal activities.

Elaine Sandhaven parked her red Porsche about a half-block away from the diner. If things went badly inside, she did not want anyone in the diner to be able to get her license number. Although she only planned to be in the diner for a short time, Elaine carefully set the car alarm; the expensive car was a tempting target for a thief.

Elaine was a tall, attractive tan brunette in her late thirties. She strode down the street confidently, but hesitated for a couple of seconds at the diner's entrance.

Mustering her resolve, she went inside and headed toward a booth in a far corner. This was Elaine's third visit to this diner. The two previous visits had merely been reconnaissance missions; today, if the opportunity presented itself, she was going to place her plan into motion.

Just a few seconds after Elaine slid into the booth, a waitress approached the table.

"Welcome back," the waitress greeted her. The waitress was a slender young woman with light brown hair.

"Thanks, Jenny," Elaine replied without glancing at the woman's name tag. Elaine had a good memory for names.

"Jenny Jawbreaker," the waitress said with a smile.

"What?" Elaine asked.

"That's not actually my last name. It is just my new name. I recently joined the local roller derby team. Now I'm Jenny Jawbreaker, but I haven't actually broken anyone's jaw yet."

Elaine laughed. "Well, have fun."

"So far it has been fun. However, I'm the least experienced player on the team, so I need lots of practice to get up to speed."

"I'm sure that you'll do well."

"Thanks. But I'm guessing that you didn't come here to hear about my roller derby adventures." Jenny placed a menu on the table. "What can I get for you today?"

"Actually, I don't need the menu. I'll just have a tuna fish salad sandwich to go. But I wanted to talk to you about something. Do you have a couple of minutes?"

Jenny glanced over her shoulder, then sat down next to Elaine in the booth. "Sure. It is pretty quiet in here now. We are between the lunch and dinner crowds."

"That's why I came here at this time of day," Elaine said with a slight grin.

"So what's up?"

"This is a very delicate matter. Can I count on your discretion?"

"Absolutely," Jenny assured her.

"Good. As you have probably guessed from our conversation during my last visit, the problem is my husband --- my soon-to-be ex-husband."

"I figured that this was about him. He must be an awful man."

"In the past couple of days, I have discovered that he is even worse than I thought when we talked previously."

"How so?"

"I know that he has been unfaithful to me, and he has been verbally and emotionally abusive, but I never considered him a violent man. However, last night he punched me in the stomach."

"That's terrible!" Jenny declared, keeping her voice down so that none of the diner's other customers or employees would hear.

"He didn't hit me in the face because he did not want anyone to see bruises on me."

"That is absolutely diabolical."

"Yes. When I married him eight years ago, I never dreamt that he would ever hit me. He seemed like such a nice, gentle man. Either he has changed very much or I never really knew him."

"What are you going to do now?"

Elaine shrugged. "For now, I have to go home and hope for the best. We have a little boy. I have to protect him. I have considered taking our son, moving to my own apartment, and getting a restraining order against my husband. However, I know that a piece of paper won't keep him from coming after me and probably killing me. I recently heard on a television news channel that many women are found murdered with restraining orders in their purses."

"I have heard the same thing," Jenny said. "I would suggest contacting the police. They might be able to help you safely get away from him."

Elaine shook her head. "No. I won't run and hide. I am going to defend myself. I want to hire someone, perhaps a private investigator, to confront him forcefully. It might even be necessary to rough him up in order for him to understand that his behavior has consequences."

"That might create some legal problems for you."

"I'm willing to take that chance. Do you know a man who could help me with this? I can pay him very well."

"I do know someone who you could talk to about this situation," Jenny said. "His name is Ch …"

At that moment Elaine's cell phone rang, cutting off Jenny in mid-word. With a look of annoyance at the interruption, Elaine pulled the phone out of her Gucci purse. She glanced at the caller ID on the phone. The annoyed expression was replaced by a surprised one.

"Jenny, would you excuse me for a minute? I have to take this call."

Jenny quickly stood up. "Of course. I'll go get your tuna fish salad sandwich." She walked toward the kitchen.

"It's about time that you returned my calls," Elaine said. "I've been leaving messages on your voice mail for a week."

"I'm sorry, Mrs. Sandhaven. I've been in the Caribbean for the past two weeks. I left my cell phone back at my condo so that I would have two weeks of peace and quiet."

"Your little Caribbean vacation almost caused you to lose a lucrative job. It almost cost you a lot of money. I was just about to hire someone else to do this job for me."

"Sounds like I called just in the nick of time."

"Hmmm. If you didn't come so highly recommended, I would tell you to get lost and hire the other man."

"Easy, Mrs. Sandhaven. I'm back now. Everything is cool. We can't discuss your case on the phone, but based on the voice mail messages that you left, I should be able to help you resolve this situation. This is the sort of case that I especially like. You'll be very pleased with its resolution."

Elaine was mollified and a satisfied grin appear on her face. "I'm glad."

"We need to meet in person."

"Yes, and as soon as possible."

"Do you know where Sister Marie Charles Park is?"

"Yes. It's on the riverfront, right off of South Broadway. At the moment I am only a few miles from there."

"Good."

"Can you meet me there in about twenty minutes?"

"That will be perfect."

"Then I'll see you there, Mrs. Sandhaven. Goodbye."

Upon seeing Elaine hang up and place her cell phone back in her purse, Jenny walked back toward the table.

"Here is you tuna fish salad sandwich, Elaine."

"Thank you, dear." Elaine paid her for the sandwich and gave her a generous tip. "As it turns out, I won't be needing the services of your friend after all. Another gentleman is going to help me resolve this situation."

"I still believe that it would be a good idea for you to speak with my friend, Elaine. He can help you. He is a very good man."

Elaine laughed as she walked away from the table. "My dear, I don't need the help of a good man. I need the help of a bad man --- a very bad man!"

She waved goodbye to Jenny and strode out of the diner.

A few minutes later Elaine was driving her Porsche down South Broadway. It was mid-afternoon and traffic was light. She drove past Bellerive Park, another small park with a good view of the Mississippi River.

She turned into the parking lot of Sister Marie Charles Park and selected a spot at the far end of the lot. Elaine was glad that there were no other cars there.

Less than a minute after she parked, a Lexus pulled onto the lot and stopped a short distance from her. A tall, athletic man in an expensive suit got out of the Lexus, strolled out onto the grass, and looked out at the river.

This has to be him, Elaine thought. She got out of her car and walked toward the man, stopping at his side.

He did not say anything. His attention seemed to be entirely focused on a barge slowly gliding down the Mississippi.

Apparently he wants me to speak first, Elaine reflected. "This park certainly has a nice view of the river," she remarked.

"Yes," he replied. "I'll have to bring my camera here sometime."

"Are you Marcus?"

"Yes, Mrs. Sandhaven." At last he turned and looked at her.

She opened her purse and pulled out a thick envelope, which she handed to him. "This envelope contains a photo of my husband and his weekly schedule. Your down payment is also in the envelope. You will receive the rest of the money after the job has been completed."

Marcus accepted the envelope and, without looking at its contents, tucked it into the inner pocket of his jacket. "You are a very well-organized person," he commented.

"Organization is the key to success."

"True. But even the best organized plans can go awry." Marcus looked toward the river again.

"So you accept the job?" Elaine asked, wary of this dangerous man.

"How did you find out about me, Mrs. Sandhaven? And how did you know how to contact me?"

"One of the computer programmers at Sandhaven Software Solutions lives in an apartment in a neighborhood that was being terrorized by a gang. Her apartment is above a small store whose owner she knows quite well. The store owner is a member of the neighborhood association that hired you to solve the gang problem. The entire neighborhood was impressed by you and grateful to you for destroying that gang."

"So the store owner told her how to contact me, and she told you?"

"That's correct. Was that okay?"

"Yes. Fine. All right, I accept the mission --- the job."

CHAPTER 4

▼

A TRIP TO THE ZOO

At about ten o'clock on Saturday morning Dennis Sandhaven came out the front door of his Central West End home. He picked up the morning paper and tossed it into the front hallway.

Marcus was waiting in his car parked near the corner. Seeing Dennis step back out onto the front porch, Marcus placed his hand on the silenced pistol that was on the seat next to him.

However, Marcus was surprised when an eight-year-old boy dashed out of the house, slamming the front door behind him. The child ran up to Dennis, and the father and son went over to their car in the driveway.

Damn, Marcus thought. His right hand moved away from the gun and back onto the steering wheel.

He followed them as they drove along Lindell Boulevard. Marcus hoped that Dennis was merely dropping the boy off somewhere, perhaps for a music lesson or at the house of one of the boy's friends.

When Dennis and his son turned into Forest Park, though, Marcus sighed, realizing that the pair probably planned to spend the day together. They parked in a lot near the zoo, and Marcus found a parking spot on the lane near the lot.

He pulled the cell phone out of his jacket pocket and called Elaine.

"Hello," she answered promptly.

"I will not kill a man in front of his child."

"I understand. I'm sorry. I didn't know that Dennis was planning on taking him out today."

"I might as well go home."

"No! I doubt that Dennis is going to spend the whole day with him. Where are they now?"

"At the zoo."

"They probably won't stay there long. Since Dennis has had a special project underway at his company, he usually goes into the office for at least a few hours on Saturday."

"My time is valuable," Marcus said.

"Yes, and that is why I am paying you very well!" Elaine snapped. "I need this situation resolved as soon as possible!" She paused and then added in a calmer voice, "Please stay with them. If you are patient, Dennis will likely drop our son off at home and then head to the office by himself. That will be your perfect opportunity."

Marcus sighed. "Very well. I don't have anything else planned, so I might as well follow them."

"Thank you, goodbye," Elaine said and hung up.

Because it was a Saturday and the weather was nice, the zoo was crowded, so Marcus was able to follow the father and son with little chance that they would notice him.

In spite of Elaine's assertion that the visit would likely be brief, Dennis and the boy spent about three hours looking at the zoo's most popular exhibits.

They walked through the River's Edge exhibit, a mythic waterway through four continents that featured many animals from around the world in a lush, natural environment. Hippos glided gracefully underwater while elephants enjoyed a waterfall above them.

At the Red Rocks exhibit, Marcus especially liked seeing the tigers, lions, and other big cats. Nearby zebras, antelope, and giraffes wandered in a natural setting.

Like me, Marcus reflected, those big cats are predators who cannot reach their prey. They are constrained by physical barriers while I am constrained by my moral code.

Marcus casually followed the pair into the Fragile Forest area featuring gorillas, chimpanzees, and orangutans in a naturalized outdoor setting. Visitors were able to look through large glass windows into the habitat furnished with tall grasses and live trees.

This zoo has certainly changed a lot through the years, Marcus thought as he recalled a childhood visit to the zoo with his father. The apes have much nicer living quarters now.

Marcus smiled as he remembered returning home and telling his mother that he wanted a gorilla for a pet. He was so insistent that she pretended to call a pet store and order a gorilla.

Chuckling at the happy memory, Marcus wandered over to the Lakeside Crossing outdoor restaurant, purchased a Pepsi, and sat drinking it while he waited.

Meanwhile, the father and son rode the Zooline Railroad over to the 1904 World's Fair Flight Cage. After walking through the huge cage and looking at the birds, they headed toward the exit with Marcus following at a distance.

When they pulled out of the zoo's parking lot, Marcus was already in his car parked on the nearby lane. He stayed about a hundred yards behind them as Dennis drove out of Forest Park. Marcus expected them to head back toward their home in the

Central West End neighborhood, but instead Dennis turned onto Highway 40 and drove east.

Where on God's earth are they going now? He speculated about their destination as he followed them across the Poplar Street Bridge over the Mississippi River into Illinois. Marcus considered turning around and driving back home to his condo, but curiosity propelled him forward. I have nothing better to do this afternoon anyway, he decided.

Dennis and his son turned onto the driveway of some attractively-landscaped grounds. Upon spotting the sign that read "Our Lady of the Snows," Marcus realized that he had arrived at Belleville's most popular tourist destination. He had never been here previously, but he had often heard about the impressive Christmas display that the Our Lady of the Snows religious shrine had every year.

Marcus chuckled with grim humor. This is getting worse and worse. Now Dennis Sandhaven is on holy ground. I won't kill anyone in the presence of a child, and I won't kill a person in a church or on holy ground.

After parking, Marcus walked past a reflecting pool with a fountain in the center. The reflecting pool also featured four large copper bells encased in Byzantine turrets that were tolling to signal the start of a new hour.

He followed Dennis and the boy as they walked through a grove of evergreens and pines. Marcus had the impression that Dennis was familiar with this place; Dennis moved with the decisiveness of a man who knew exactly where he was going.

Numerous other persons were also heading in the same direction, apparently heading toward the same event. As he came over the crest of a hill, Marcus saw that a priest had begun leading visitors along the fourteen Stations of the Cross. Each station had a hand-painted background scene that provided a realistic, three-dimensional effect.

Dennis and his son joined the other visitors as they followed the priest from station to station. As the group proceeded down the path, at each station the priest would say some prayers, then provide some personal reflections.

"Saint Alphonsus Liguori teaches us that 'God is very ready to give us His help, but we must ask for it in prayer. It is the lantern which lights our way to eternity.'

"I recently read a book entitled **The Reed of God** by Caryll Houselander, who comments upon the Book of Revelation written by St. John the Evangelist. Houselander writes that John saw Mary 'standing in heaven, clothed in the sun and with her feet upon the moon. Facing the sun, she received its light and gave it back as the moon does.'"

"Using another image, Houselander writes that Mary 'was a reed through which the Eternal Love was to be piped as a shepherd's song.'"

When the group arrived at the station depicting Veronica wiping the face of Jesus, the priest said, "Just as the holy face of Jesus was imprinted onto Veronica's cloth, we need to have his face imprinted upon our souls."

As they reached the final station in which Jesus was placed in the tomb, the priest said, "A couple of years ago I heard a Franciscan priest at St. Anthony of Padua parish in South St. Louis talk about a reverse Stations of the Cross. This priest had once seen a nun do the stations in reverse order, beginning with this one. He had never previously seen anyone do this and was fascinated. When the priest asked the nun why she did the stations in reverse order, the nun replied that Mary had to walk home after watching her son be crucified. In all likelihood, she walked back into Jerusalem along the same road that Jesus had carried the cross. So this nun would reflect upon what Mary might have been thinking as she arrived at each station."

At the conclusion of the Stations of the Cross, Dennis and his son wandered the grounds for a few minutes, then returned to their car. Apparently attending this religious ceremony was the main purpose for their visit here today, Marcus realized.

He watched them drive away, but he did not follow. There was no reason. He was already fairly certain that he was not going to kill Dennis Sandhaven. Perhaps I will test his character before I make a final decision, Marcus thought. In any case, I will never again accept any assignment as a hit man. I'm tired of all the killing. I'm going to become just a regular private detective.

Marcus sat in his car for another fifteen minutes, soaking in the peaceful atmosphere of the place.

CHAPTER 5

▼

THE DEFENDER

Later that evening at about nine o'clock, Dennis Sandhaven emerged from a Walgreens on Grand Avenue, carrying his bag of purchases.

An apparently-homeless man in a navy blue hoodie approached Dennis. "Sir, could you spare a few dollars?"

Dennis reached into his pocket and pulled out a twenty dollar bill, which he handed to the man. "Here you go. Good luck to you."

"Thank you, sir. I promise that I won't spend the money on drugs or alcohol. I've just had a bit of bad luck."

"I understand. Life can be hard sometimes." Dennis took another twenty and gave it to the man. "I hope that your luck gets better. God bless you."

"God bless you, too, sir," the man said as he and Dennis headed in opposite directions on the sidewalk.

Almost as soon as he rounded the corner, Marcus Augustine spotted a truly-homeless man holding a large can as he asked persons for money.

"This is for you, friend." Marcus took the forty dollars that Dennis had just given him and dropped both twenty dollar bills into the man's can.

"Thank you so much!" the surprised man declared. "You are a good man."

Marcus laughed heartily as he continued on his way down the street.

The next morning Elaine, carrying a cup of coffee, stepped out onto the parking lot of a fast-food restaurant.

Marcus suddenly appeared in front of her, startling her so much that she almost spilled the hot coffee.

"Damn! How do you do that?"

Marcus grinned. "I can't give away my secrets, Mrs. Sandhaven."

"I guess not." Elaine managed a smile. "When any other person says that if he tells you his secret, he will have to kill you, he is joking. However, I don't suppose that you would be joking about it."

"I'm not much for jokes these days."

Elaine looked around in order to make sure that no one else was within hearing distance. "Speaking of killing persons, I was wondering why my husband is still alive. He left the house just a couple of minutes before I did."

"And your husband is going to remain alive. I have decided not to kill him."

Elaine was taken aback. "Why not?"

"Because you lied to me. I don't believe that he is an abusive husband. You heard that I only kill bad persons, so you concocted a story so that I would accept the assignment."

Joseph P. Rogers   35

"How can you be so sure that he is not evil?" Elaine demanded. "I can show you bruises."

"Bruises prove nothing. I have a bruise on my hip from bumping into a table in the dark a couple of nights ago."

"He beats me!" Elaine insisted. "Why else would I want him killed?"

Marcus looked at her intently. "Now you have asked an interesting question. That is a question to which I would like to know the answer. I might know the answer, but I will admit that I am not certain."

She glared at him. "What do believe the answer is?"

"You want your husband dead because you want to inherit his company. If you divorce him, you will get a nice settlement, perhaps almost half of his money. However, you won't get Sandhaven Software Solutions. He will remain in control of the company. This is all about money, your greed for more money."

"That is ridiculous," Elaine said.

Marcus was surprised that Elaine seemed to relax slightly. She thought that I was going to say something else, Marcus realized. What is going on here? I will need to play another card or two in order to get her to reveal her hand.

"I read the *Wall Street Journal* every day," he said. "It is my favorite newspaper. As you might imagine, I earn good money in this profession. I want to invest it wisely. Yesterday I read a *Wall Street Journal* story that mentioned Sandhaven Software was working with a computer software computer owned by Douglas Neldt, the man who was assassinated last week. Then a bomb destroyed most of Neldt's company."

Elaine's eyes narrowed. "So what?"

"So that's quite a coincidence. For better or for worse, the death of Neldt and the destruction of his company will have a profound effect on Sandhaven Software. Financial analysts believe that if Sandhaven Software is able to successfully complete the

Intelligent Agency program, the value of the company could double or triple."

"You have no idea of the danger in which you are placing yourself," Elaine hissed. "It would be better for you if you had neglected to read your *Wall Street Journal* that day."

"Do not forgot who I am or what I do, Mrs. Sandhaven. It is not wise to threaten me."

"You are a fool who has stumbled into a world unknown to you. You are wandering into territory to which you have no map."

"Then enlighten me. Tell me what is going on."

"No."

Marcus could see that the woman was very tense. I am getting close to the truth, he reasoned, but there is something going on here that I don't understand. A new idea occurred to him, and he decided to play another card.

"Did you have something to do with the assassination of Douglas Neldt?" Marcus asked.

For several seconds, Elaine stared at him in silence.

"I'll assume that means 'yes.' Who did you hire to kill Neldt?"

"You are the king of fools. Walk away now if you wish to live."

"I want answers."

"If you are unwilling to kill my husband, so be it. I will hire someone else to kill him."

"Your husband will not be harmed. He is a good man. And your son clearly loves his father. How could you be so heartless? Don't you realize the grief that you would cause your son?"

"That is my concern. Leave now. I never want to see you or hear from you again."

"Understand this, Mrs. Sandhaven: your husband is under my protection."

"You must be kidding!" she declared.

"You will not hire another hit man nor will you kill him yourself. Do not even think about poisoning him. If he is killed or dies of mysterious causes, I will send the police a complete report about you. I might even decide to pay you a visit myself."

"You might not be alive long enough to do so."

"Mrs. Sandhaven, I was a sniper with special forces in Afghanistan. Once I got separated from the rest of my platoon in a town controlled by the Taliban. At one point in the evening, I found myself matched against four Taliban snipers on adjacent buildings. All four were quite determined to kill me. However, by the end of the evening, I had killed all four Taliban snipers, and I walked out of the town in good health."

"You are certainly a proud man. It's time that someone taught you some humility."

"That might be true. It is probably the first true thing that you have said to me." Marcus walked toward his car. "Goodbye, Mrs. Sandhaven."

As he got into the Lexus, she continued to stand there, glaring coldly at him. Finally, after about thirty seconds, she went over to her own car and drove away.

Staying about two blocks behind her car, Marcus followed Elaine. It is very curious that she did not ask for a refund of the money that she paid me. She did not care about several thousand dollars. Perhaps money is not the motivation for wanting her husband killed.

If not money, what is the motive? Marital infidelity? His or hers? No. It is too much of a coincidence that Douglas Neldt was killed just days ago.

It appears that she is driving toward Sandhaven Software Solutions. That is probably where I can find an answer. I will slip into the building and do a bit of exploration.

CHAPTER 6

▼

FATIMA'S TALE

Fatima Cedars was a petite woman with short hair and a perfect olive complexion upon which many persons commented. Many also noticed the serene expression that was usual for her countenance. Lately, though, Fatima's inner tranquility was being tested by a challenging situation at her workplace.

Fatima knew that there was something wrong at Sandhaven Software Solutions. Something was very wrong.

She had worked at the company for almost a year. Fatima had been hired by Elaine Sandhaven when Elaine had made a recruiting trip to the Middle East and visited Fatima's university in Lebanon. Elaine had been very impressed by the young woman who ranked near the top of her university class.

After moving to St. Louis, Fatima had found an apartment near her workplace. The first three months on the job had gone well, and she enjoyed the intellectually challenging work. Using the simulation software, she designed clever viruses that provided a rigorous test for the Intelligent Agency program that attempted to destroy her viruses.

However, her relationships with her coworkers gradually deteriorated. The company employees were divided into cliques based on ethnicity and religion. At first Fatima was befriended by the other Muslim employees, but her lack of adherence to traditional Islamic practices eventually caused a rift with most of the other Muslims at the company.

Fatima had grown up in Turkey and attended colleges in Croatia and Lebanon. Although she still considered herself a Muslim, she dressed like an American woman and liked many aspects of western culture.

In the evenings, she liked to go dancing in the Bosnian nightclubs on Gravois Avenue near the famous Bevo Mill restaurant that was located in a windmill. She felt comfortable with the Bosnian Muslims and their European culture. The Bosnian immigrants had infused a new life and energy into the midtown area.

Fatima wished that her days were as pleasant as her evenings. At least the work here is intriguing, she consoled herself as she sat alone in the cafeteria.

Some employees at the company only spoke in Arabic to each other so that the Americans would not understand what they were saying. Fatima spoke fluent Arabic, and some of the conversations that she overheard disturbed her. Some of them were extreme fundamentalists who clearly hated the United States. These extremists apparently were occasionally having secret meetings in a conference room at Sandhaven Software.

For the past week Fatima had been working late every day on a secret assignment. Shortly after the murders of Douglas Neldt and Rebecca Wright, Dennis Sandhaven had given Fatima the task of helping to rebuild the Intelligent Agency program.

A couple programmers who had survived the explosions at Neldt's company had also been given remote access to the mainframe computer at Sandhaven Software. Fatima had never seen either of these programmers; they were working from a hidden location in Maryland where they were in protective custody.

Shortly after seven o'clock that evening, Fatima disconnected her laptop computer from the mainframe, then logged off. She folded the laptop closed and left her office, weary from the long workday and anxious to stop by a fast-food restaurant for dinner. As she locked her office door, she debated whether to go to Kentucky Fried Chicken, McDonald's, or Lion's Choice.

"Working late again, Fatima?" A woman's voice came from behind her.

Fatima turned and was surprised to see Elaine Sandhaven walking down the hallway toward her.

"Yes, Mrs. Sandhaven."

"What are you working on?"

Fatima hesitated. Apparently Dennis had not told his wife about the secret assignment. Fatima wondered why he had not told his wife. She decided that it would be wise to be discrete.

"Is something wrong?" The tall woman loomed over Fatima, who suddenly felt ill at ease.

"No, nothing is wrong. I'm just catching up on some projects that have fallen behind schedule." Fatima started to walk around her, but Elaine moved to block her path. Fatima looked up at her. "It has been a long day, Mrs. Sandhaven, and I'm very tired. I want to get home."

"We all want to get home, Fatima, but there is important work that needs to be done."

Boutros Mahdi and Rashid Fuad walked into the hallway. Fatima suspected that they had been listening from around the corner.

Elaine glanced back over her shoulder at the two men. "Just a few minutes ago, the three of us were discussing some important topics. There are many things wrong back in your homeland, Fatima. Do you ever think about your people? Do you ever think about anything besides yourself?"

Fatima had never seen this side of this woman with whom she had only spoken briefly on a couple of occasions. "Good evening, Mrs. Sandhaven," Fatima said, moving around her.

The two men blocked her from moving further down the hallway.

"Good evening to you, too," Fatima said to the men, who continued to stand there and did not seemed inclined to move. "That means get out of my way!" she added tersely.

"We need to talk to you," Boutros said, glancing down at the laptop computer that Fatima held. "We need access to the Intelligent Agency project. We are going to help rebuild the program."

"I will need to check with Dennis Sandhaven before I can give you access," Fatima said. "You need top-secret clearance to work on Intelligent Agency."

"They have clearance," Elaine said. "Dennis wants them to have access. Give them your laptop computer, Fatima, and get them logged onto the mainframe."

"I'm sorry, Mrs. Sandhaven, but I will first need to discuss this with your husband."

"Are you calling me a liar?"

"No. I am saying that there is an established procedure for how things must be done. We must follow security protocols."

"If you disobey my orders, you will be fired!" Elaine shouted at her. "And if you are fired, you will be deported!"

"That's not true!" Fatima declared, then darted past the two men.

She had caught them off-guard, and she dashed down another hallway that led to the parking lot. However, before she reached the exit door, Rashid caught her and shoved her forcefully against the wall.

"What is your hurry, little Fatima? Are you anxious to get to your nightclub? Are some of your American friends waiting for you?"

Boutros stepped forward and grabbed her by the hair. "You are going to give us that computer and log us in now."

"No!"

With both arms, she pressed the laptop against her body while the two men tried to pry it away from her.

Rashid raised his arm to strike her, but he never got a chance. Seemingly out of nowhere, Marcus Augustine sprang forward and grabbed Rashid's arm, twisting it all the way back, breaking the arm. Rashid collapsed to the floor in pain.

Boutros threw a punch at Marcus, but Marcus easily blocked the punch, grabbed Boutros by the hair, and slammed him face first into the soda machine with such force that the vending machine almost tipped over. Half-conscious, his nose broken and his face bloody, Boutros fell next to his friend on the floor.

Elaine, who had been watching from the end of the hallway, exchanged momentary eye contact with Marcus. Then she turned the corner and hurried away.

"Who are you?" Fatima asked her rescuer.

"I'm a man who doesn't like to be deceived. Come with me. We need to get out of here."

Fatima followed Marcus out of the side door. They paused out on the parking lot.

"I think that those people are terrorists!" Fatima exclaimed. "They might be Al Qaeda . I have been working with terrorists!"

"I believe that you are correct; they are either Al Qaeda or some similar group. And it is too dangerous for you to go back to your apartment. They will go there searching for you."

"What can I do?"

"You'll need to go into hiding temporarily. I have a place where you can stay."

"What is your name?"

"My name is Marcus Augustine. I'm a private detective. It's a long story that I will tell you later." He pointed toward his Lexus. "I'm parked over there. Follow me in your car. Don't worry."

As she pulled out her car keys, she called to him, "I feel safe with you. Thank you for helping me."

"I'm glad to be of service," Marcus said, getting into his car.

With Fatima following close behind, he drove to his condominium in Clayton. After walking her to the front door, Marcus handed her the key to the condo.

"I would suggest that you call your boss, Dennis Sandhaven, and tell him what happened at the company this evening. He needs to be on guard against his wife and some of his employees."

"Yes, I'll tell him everything."

"Call from your cell phone. You can tell him everything except that you are staying here. You can trust him, but his phone might be bugged or his wife might be eavesdropping on him. Let everyone assume that you are returning to your apartment."

"I am hoping that I can return to my apartment!"

"You should be able to return soon. One way or another, this matter will likely be resolved within the next few days. After what I heard at the software company today, I have a better idea what is going on. Until a couple of hours ago, I mistakenly thought that this was all about money. Now I realize that Elaine Sandhaven and her comrades don't care about money at all."

"They are fanatics! Extremists!" Fatima exclaimed.

Marcus nodded. "They are the same enemy that I fought in Afghanistan. However, now they are here. I suppose that they have always been here."

Meanwhile, Elaine drove away from the software company, angry and frustrated by Marcus's intervention. *How dare he! Why did I ever hire that man?*

Elaine then remembered her conversation with Jenny, the waitress at the diner. *When Marcus returned my call, Jenny was about to give me the contact information for some man named Chuck. I should have hired Chuck to kill Dennis.*

Elaine pulled onto a side street where she parked while she fumbled through her purse in search of the scrap of paper on which she had written Jenny's phone number. *If I can't find that number, I suppose I could just drive over to the diner. Oh, wait, I have always spoken to Jenny there in the afternoon; I don't know whether she works in the evening. That diner might not even be open this late in the evening.*

Found it! Elaine pulled the scrap of paper out of her purse. Using her cell phone, she called the number. After a few seconds, Jenny answered.

"Hello?" There was a lot of noise in the background.

"Jenny? This is Elaine. I can barely hear you."

"Hi, Elaine. I'm at roller derby. We don't start for another twenty minutes, but most of the crowd is already here."

"They are quite noisy."

"Yes. Hold on a second. I'm skating toward the exit door. I will be able to hear you better outside."

When Jenny got outside, she asked, "Can you hear me better now?"

"Yes. That's much better."

"I can only talk for a minute. I will need start getting ready for the match."

"I won't keep you. I just need the phone number of that man named Chuck. The guy that I hired proved to be unsatisfactory, so I'd like to hire Chuck for that special project that we discussed."

After a momentary pause, Jenny said, "I'll need to talk to Chuck first to make sure that it is all right to give you his number."

"That's fine, Elaine, but this matter is rather urgent. I need to speak with Chuck as soon as possible."

"I understand. I'll tell him right now. He's here to watch my roller derby bout. He arrived just a few minutes ago."

"Excellent. I can come there to speak with him."

"First I need to find him in the crowd; there are several hundred persons here. I'll give him your number and ask him to call you as soon as he can."

"Thanks, Jenny. And I'm sure that you understand this situation requires the utmost discretion. Please don't mention this to anyone else."

"You can count on my discretion."

"Thank you. I'll be waiting for Chuck's call."

"You'll be hearing from him soon. Bye, Elaine."

After hanging up, Jenny went back inside. For about fifteen seconds, she scanned the crowd, then spotted her friend over at the souvenir stand. Jenny skated over to him, and he glanced over his shoulder at her.

"Hey, look what I just bought." He held up three photos of her in her Jenny Jawbreaker uniform. "I'm going to need these autographed later. I don't want to slow you down now, though. Your teammates are already out there warming up. You probably should join them."

"I will in a minute. But I have some news. Guess who I just got a call from?"

"If you wait for me to guess correctly, it will be a lot longer than a minute before you get to your warm-up. In fact, the match will probably be over before I correctly guess who called you."

She laughed. "You might be right. I'd better just tell you. Elaine, that woman from the diner, just called me."

"Oh, really, what did she want?"

"She wants to hire you to help her with her husband problem. Apparently she hired some guy who failed to help her. She did not provide any details."

"What does she want me to do?"

"I'm not sure, but she is very anxious to speak with you. She wants to come here this evening."

"Wow. That is short notice."

"Will you talk to her?"

"I suppose. However, I won't like missing some of your roller derby game."

"You'll see most of it. Anyway I'm not very good yet. This is just my rookie season."

"Your rookie season? Are you planning on continuing for a second season?"

"Maybe. We'll see."

"Hmmm. That's interesting."

"Hey, I really need to start warming up." She handed her cell phone to him. "And you need to call her -- she is freaking out. You can use my phone. I don't want to take it all the way back to the locker room, and I don't want to have it on me during the game. It could get smashed. Her number is the most recent incoming call."

"Okay. Good luck with your game."

"Thanks. Good luck with your meeting with Elaine." With a wave, she skated away to join her teammates, who were skating in casual laps around the rink where the bout would begin in three minutes.

Anticipating the start of the game, the noise of the crowd was gradually increasing. Like Jenny had done a short while ago, Chuck decided to go outside so that he could hear better.

As soon as the exit door closed behind him, he made the call.

"Hello," Elaine answered. "Jenny?"

"No. This is Chuck, her friend. Jenny let me borrow her phone. She said that you wanted to speak with me."

"Yes, I'm very anxious to speak with you. Would it be possible for you to meet with me in a few minutes?"

"Yes, that will be fine."

"Thank you. Actually, I'm only a couple of minutes from your location right now. I'm about to turn off Lindbergh Boulevard. Right after I spoke with Jenny, I started driving toward the sports complex where the roller derby game is being held."

"Good. I'll meet you in front of the building. What type of car are you driving?"

"A red Porsche."

"Okay, I will meet you out front."

Chuck was standing at the side of the sports complex, which also included an ice hockey rink. He walked around to the front of the building.

After seeing a red Porsche pull into a parking space, Chuck approached the woman getting out of the car.

"Elaine?"

"Yes." She shook hands with him. "And you must be Chuck."

"Right."

"Has Jenny told you about my problem?"

"Yes. I was sorry to hear that your husband has been abusive."

"Extremely abusive. I'm in fear for my life."

"That's very unfortunate. There are some agencies that can help you with that abusive situation."

She frowned and shook her head. "No, they can't help me. My husband is going to kill me unless I stop him first. I'm counting on you to help me, Chuck. I need your special services."

For a fraction of a second, Elaine thought that she saw a look of surprise on his face. As quickly as it appeared, though, the surprised expression vanished and was replaced by a pleasant, inquisitive expression.

"How can I be of service?" he asked.

"I assumed that you knew why you are here. I must have my husband killed before he kills me. Are you willing to do this for me?"

"I can take care of the matter," Chuck assured her.

"Good. A couple of days ago I hired another man, but he wimped out on me. I need your assurance that you will follow this through to completion."

"I won't wimp out," he said. "I complete what I begin."

She smiled and nodded. "You seem like a very capable man. I'm glad that Jenny told me about you."

"Thank you."

"I suppose that we had better get the matter of payment out of the way," she said. "I can pay you five thousand dollars now and ten thousand after the job is completed. Is that acceptable?"

"Yes, that will be fine."

"I will need this job to completed as soon as possible," Elaine said emphatically. She discreetly handed him a manila envelope that contained the money, David Sandhaven's photo, and some information about him. "This envelope has everything that you need."

After conversing for another minute, Elaine said good-bye to Chuck and drove away. He watched her depart, then walked back into the sports complex where the flat-track roller derby bout was underway.

Jenny's team, clad in violet and gold, was engaged in a close game against the opposing team, which wore red and black uniforms. Jenny was currently winning points for her team by serving as the "jammer," the one scoring position. The jammer on each team was easy to spot because of the star worn on her helmet.

Although she had little roller derby experience, Jenny was a good skater. Over the past few years, she often skated on Grant's Trail, which ran through the suburbs of South County and eventually connected to the River des Peres bike trail.

Because the traditional quad roller skates with two wheels in the front and two wheels in the back were very stable, Jenny preferred them to the inline rollerblade skates that were faster. Jenny was glad that roller derby continued to use the quad skates rather than rollerblades.

Jenny was such a good skater that her team gave her the jammer position. In this evening's game, Jenny made her way through the pack. Her teammates, serving as blockers, tried to clear a path for her, while the opposing team attempted to knock her out of bounds.

Chuck was amused by the colorful nicknames selected by the skaters on the two teams. His friend, Jenny Jawbreaker, was protected by her teammates: Lethal Lauren, Casey Crusher, Julie Juggernaut, and Denise the Menace. On the opposing team, Sarah Slayer, Vicky Vendetta, Beth the Bruiser, Sue Smasher, and Danielle Destroyer sought to stop Jenny so that their own jammer could begin to win points for their team.

During the intermission between the second and third periods, one of the referees put on a demonstration of his skating proficiency. The highlight of the performance was his impressive jump over seven volunteers, all of whom were very glad that the referee's jump was successful.

At the conclusion of the game, which Jenny's team won by a narrow margin, Chuck signaled to Jenny, who skated over toward the bleachers, where the two of them conferred privately about his conversation with Elaine. After making plans for the next day, Chuck congratulated Jenny on her excellent skating and on her team's victory.

CHAPTER 7

▼

HEROES UNMASKED

Shortly after traveling over the Missouri River and entering St. Charles County, Dennis Sandhaven exited Highway 70 at 5th Street. Two large signs presented him with the attractive options of either going right toward a riverboat casino or left to the Bass Pro Shop, a huge outdoor recreational products store that included a large aquarium.

Dennis turned right toward the river, but he drove past the casino entrance and onto the cobblestone streets of downtown St. Charles.

Chuck's car was never more than a quarter-mile behind him. In spite of his line of work, Chuck had not often covertly followed persons, and he did not consider himself especially adept at it. However, the idea that someone might be following him had not occurred to Dennis, so he did not notice Chuck.

Dennis went into a restaurant and had dinner with two business associates. Sitting on a bench outside the restaurant, Chuck patiently waited. He enjoyed people-watching as hundreds of persons went in and out of shops along this popular shopping and dining district. Chuck made a brief phone call to Jenny as they coordinated their plans.

When he finally emerged from the restaurant, Dennis said good-bye to his two colleagues and strolled casually down toward the park that ran along the riverfront.

Dennis paused to look at a statue honoring Meriwether Lewis and William Clark and their historic Lewis and Clark expedition that traveled along the Missouri River, going against the current the entire way.

There were a few fishermen scattered along the banks of the river. After looking at the Lewis and Clark statue, Dennis had strolled over to speak with one of the fishermen.

Chuck slowly walked toward Dennis. After he finishes his conversation with the fisherman, he will be alone, and it will be the perfect time to approach him, Chuck realized.

"I'm probably scaring off all the fish with all my talking," Dennis told the older man to whom he had been speaking. "I'd better be on my way. Good luck with your fishing."

The two men said goodbye, and Dennis wandered away from the riverbank toward a copse of trees. Now is my chance, Chuck thought as he walked rapidly toward Dennis.

"Hello, Mr. Sandhaven," Chuck said. "May I speak with you for a moment?"

As Chuck's right hand reached into his jacket, he felt the barrel of a gun pressed against his back.

"That hand better be empty as you take it out," Marcus warned from behind Chuck. "Keep both of your hands at your side and walk slowly toward that tree."

"Who are you?" Chuck asked.

"I am Marcus. Your boss might have mentioned me to you. I'm the guy that she hired before she hired you. I will be interested to hear what lies she told you." Marcus reached into Chuck's jacket and took Chuck's pistol out of his shoulder holster. "You won't be needing that gun."

"I wasn't reaching for the gun," Chuck said calmly. "I was reaching for my identification in order to show it to Mr. Sandhaven. I did not intend to harm him."

"Right. Tell me some other stories," Marcus said.

"I'm a good storyteller," Chuck said. "What story would you like to hear?"

"You're Mister Funnyman. I actually don't need any stories right now." Marcus glanced over at Dennis. "Mr. Sandhaven, you did a good job drawing this guy out into the open."

"Thank you for calling me when I was in the restaurant," Dennis said. "And thank you for helping Fatima."

"I'm glad to be of service." Marcus returned his attention to Chuck. "Tell me, Mr. Funnyman, what is your real name?"

"My name is Charles Valentine."

"Okay, Charles, besides killing people, what do you do for a living?"

"Is that what you think I'm here to do?"

It suddenly occurred to Marcus that this Charles Valentine was stalling. The idea occurred to him a moment too late to take action. Jenny had been moving swiftly and silently along the grass of the riverside park. Marcus had not heard her approach.

"Drop your gun," she said as she pressed the barrel of her own gun against Marcus's neck.

"What goes around comes around, I suppose," Marcus said. He quickly calculated his odds of successfully knocking her gun aside without being shot. Even though he could move very fast, Marcus did not like the odds.

As if reading his mind, Jenny said, "I have never shot anyone, and I would prefer not to shoot you. It would be better for both of us if you drop that gun."

"If you kill me, I will kill your friend," Marcus said, keeping his pistol against Chuck's back.

"He is my friend and my partner," Jenny said. "Perhaps this will help you make the right decision." With the gun still in her right hand, she pulled out the leather case containing her badge and held the badge forward so that he could see it. "I am Lieutenant Jennifer Halloran, a detective with the St. Louis Police Department. And the gentleman in front of you is Lieutenant Charles Valentine."

"Oh." Marcus made his decision and lowered his gun.

"Drop it," Jenny ordered, and he did so.

Charlie Valentine turned around, picked up Marcus's gun from the ground, and placed the gun into his pocket. He took a pair of handcuffs out of his jacket and started to place the handcuffs on Marcus.

"No, wait!" Dennis Sandhaven implored. "Please don't arrest him. This man did not know that you were a police detective. He thought that you were a hit man hired by my wife to kill me. We have been communicating by cell phones. He was keeping an eye on me in order to protect me. When he spotted you following me, he told me to walk over near the river so that he could trap you. We both thought that you were a hit man."

"That was a reasonable assumption," Charlie acknowledged, placing the handcuffs back into his jacket. "Elaine Sandhaven did hire me to kill you. Lieutenant Halloran and I have been on an undercover assignment for several weeks."

"We will need to see some identification," Jenny said to Marcus.

"Here is my driver's license and my private investigator's license," Marcus said, taking the two cards out of his wallet and handing them to her.

She examined them for a few seconds, then gave both cards to Charlie.

After looking at the two licenses, Charlie returned them to Marcus. "I have heard of you previously," Charlie said.

"I have heard of you, too." Jenny looked at Marcus intently. "You have been questioned about a couple of murders, but you've never been arrested. There was never been enough evidence to arrest you."

"I'm as innocent as a lamb, of course," Marcus asserted.

"Undoubtedly," Charlie said. "How did you get involved in this situation?"

"A few days ago I returned from a Caribbean cruise, and there was a voice mail message from Elaine Sandhaven. I went to meet her at a small park overlooking the Mississippi --- Sister Marie Charles Park. She told me that her husband had been physically abusive. She said that she feared for her life ..."

"That was a lie that she told you!" Dennis interrupted. "I have never hit her or threatened her. In fact, until a few weeks ago, we got along very well."

"What happened to change things?" Jenny asked.

"One evening Elaine got a phone call. I was sitting on the couch reading the newspaper. While she was on the phone, I noticed that she said very little, and she became very pale. After she hung up, I asked Elaine about to whom she was speaking. She said that it was a call that she hoped that she would never receive. She refused to tell me anything else. The next day she became very cold and remote toward me."

"That's very strange," Charlie said. "Marcus, let's get back to your involvement. You were telling us about your conversation with Mrs. Sandhaven in the park."

"Well, to make a long story short, she hired me, and the next day I followed Mr. Sandhaven. I suspected that his wife had been lying to me. Then, yesterday I went to Sandhaven Software in order to try to find out what was really going on. I parked in the back lot because I wanted to slip into a side door. I did not want to have to pass by the receptionist in the front lobby because I had no legitimate reason to be there.

"As I walked across the parking lot, I noticed several employees gathered near a door as they smoked cigarettes. I pretended to make a cell phone call and casually walked toward them. When I was close enough to hear, I noticed that they were speaking Arabic. I was with the special forces in Afghanistan for about five years, and I speak Arabic fairly well.

"In any case, they did not pay any attention to me. They had no idea that I was listening to them or that I could understand what they were saying --- at least most of what they were saying. They were speaking a little too fast for me to catch everything. However, I got the impression that they were Islamic extremists who were enthusiastic about the idea of jihad against America.

"After a few minutes, I figured that they were going to get suspicious if I stayed out there any longer, so I went through the door that they had left ajar so that they could get back inside. I'm guessing that the door is usually kept locked from the outside."

"Didn't anyone question you about why you were going inside?" Jenny asked.

"No, I just tried to look relaxed and confident; I walked with authority like my presence there was a normal, everyday thing. I started to look around the building, but I didn't find any additional information. There were many persons around, and they were wearing employee identification badges. I narrowly dodged a security guard. I knew that another guard or employee would eventually stop and question me, so I hid in the janitor's closet.

"I decided to stay there until most of the employees had gone home. In the early evening, I emerged from the closet and went into the hallway. There were still a few persons in the building, but I didn't have any trouble avoiding them. While I was exploring the place, I heard the sound of an argument, then saw a young lady running down a hallway with two men in pursuit.

"I recognized the two men as two of the Islamic extremists that I had seen outside earlier that day. They grabbed the young woman and were about to beat her when I intervened. I became very angry and gave them what they deserved. I gave the one man a good view of the inside of a vending machine, and I broke the arm of the other man in a very unpleasant way.

"Then I took the young lady named Fatima Cedars outside. We each got in our cars, and she followed me to my condo in Clayton. I knew that it would not be safe for her to return to her apartment, so I told her that she could stay in my condo. Fatima has the whole place to herself because I am currently living at my house in Creve Coeur."

"You own both a condo in Clayton and a house in Creve Coeur," Jenny remarked. "The private detective business must be very profitable."

"It has its ups and downs," Marcus said pleasantly.

"Fatima called me from his condo," Dennis Sandhaven interjected. "She told me everything that had happened. Naturally, I was shocked, but I now understood why Elaine had been acting so strange since receiving that phone call a couple of weeks ago."

"Apparently she was a sleeper agent for the terrorists," Charlie said. "She had probably been waiting for that phone call for years --- waiting to be called to action."

"Yes," Dennis said. "My first priority was to ensure the safety of our son. I didn't think that she would harm him, but obviously I never really knew the woman. Perhaps she would have used him as a hostage. In any case, I took my son to my sister's house and explained the situation to her. Two hours later she and my son went to the airport and left on a flight to Florida.

"Then Fatima called me again and arranged for me to meet Marcus. He drove me to Sandhaven Software and served as my bodyguard during the hour that I was there. I fired Boutros Mahdi and Rashid Fuad, and I cancelled their badges and computer passwords. I also deleted Elaine's computer password, and I informed the security guards that she should not be allowed into the building.

"Once I finished doing everything possible to stop Elaine and her co-conspirators, I took my computer and all of the Intelligent Agency documentation with me to the Holiday Inn on Hampton. I decided to get a room there because it is close to Sandhaven Software, but no one knows that I am there."

"That should be a safe enough location as long as you don't tell anyone that you are there," Jenny said.

"Lieutenant Valentine, I'm very curious about how you tricked Elaine Sandhaven into believing that you were a hit man," Marcus said.

"Well, my partner here actually deserves the credit," Charlie said. "For several weeks, Jenny has been working undercover at a diner called Angie's Place. Ever since that diner opened, criminals have liked to use it as a meeting place, so the police department likes to keep an eye on it."

"In the past few months, there have been a number of instances of identity theft. Five members of the local roller derby team had their identities stolen. They frequently ate lunch or dinner at Angie's Place, so we suspected that either an employee or regular customer of Angie's Place might be responsible for the identity thefts.

"I've always been pretty good at roller skating," Jenny continued, "so I joined the roller derby team. We also thought that it was possible that someone on the team was stealing her teammate's personal information and credit card numbers. By getting on the team, I could conduct an investigation from the inside."

"Jenny had both possibilities covered," Charlie said. "If the identity thefts were occurring at the diner, she was a waitress there. If the identity thefts happened in the team locker room, Jenny Jawbreaker was on the team and watching everyone."

"So did you catch the culprit?" Marcus asked.

"Yes," Jenny replied. "Yesterday evening I was keeping an eye on a waiter named Hassar Bahar. I thought that his behavior was suspicious. Whenever a customer paid with a credit card, Hassar always took much too long to complete the transaction. Yesterday I caught him using an electronic device to copy all of the information from the credit card, so I arrested him on the spot."

"I checked with some of the other ladies on the roller derby team, and they said that Hassar had frequently been their waiter when they ate at the diner. Apparently that was when the identity thefts occurred."

"While we were booking him at the station, we did a background check," Charlie said. "It turns out that he has been a person of interest to the FBI for quite a while. Hassar Bahar has close ties to several Islamic extremist groups including Al Qaeda."

"We contacted the FBI and spoke with an agent named David Hummel," Jenny added. "He suspects that the terrorists might be doing identity theft in order to provide false identities to terrorists."

"Perhaps Hassar Bahar is working with Elaine and Boutros Mahdi and Rashid Fuad!" Dennis exclaimed.

"That's possible," Charlie acknowledged. "In fact, David Hummel and his partner, Sam Troutman, are on their way to St. Louis right now. They will be surprised to hear about these latest events at Sandhaven Software."

"All the events seem to be converging in St. Louis," Jenny said. "Just like the Missouri River and the Mississippi River."

"'Where the rivers meet, DeSmet began,'" Charlie said.

"You lost me on that one," Jenny said.

"Oh, that is a quote on a statue on St. Louis University's campus. It refers to the Jesuit missionary, Father Pierre DeSmet, who began his missionary journey near the junction of the two rivers."

"This historical moment brought to you by Charlie Valentine," Jenny laughed. She glanced over at Marcus. "We are going to need to speak with Fatima Cedars and take her into protective custody," Jenny told him. "Perhaps we could follow you to your condo."

"That will be fine."

"I'm sure that the two FBI agents are also going to want to meet with you, Mr. Sandhaven. We are going to pick them up at the airport later this evening."

Jenny, Charlie, Dennis, and Marcus walked out of the riverside park, crossed a cobblestone street, and headed toward their cars in the parking lots.

CHAPTER 8

▼

MATCHMAKER, MATCHMAKER

Charlie and Jenny drove toward the house belonging to Violet and Gregory Valentine, making a quick stop at a neighborhood grocery store along the way.

"Chuck," he repeated the nickname that he had used for their undercover work, an amused expression on his face. "I haven't been called that in a long time."

"I've always liked the name 'Chuck.' There was a nice guy named Chuck in my class in grade school. And, in the **Peanuts** comics, Peppermint Patty always called Charlie Brown 'Chuck.'"

He laughed. "Okay. You win. I'll be 'Chuck' for a while."

"That sounds good to me, Chuck."

"So, Jenny Jawbreaker, are you enjoying roller derby?"

"It's fun. In fact, I've decided to continue doing it even after this charade is over."

"Really?" he laughed. "That's great!"

"Are you sure that your brother and sister-in-law won't mind me joining all of you for dinner?" Jenny asked.

"No, they won't mind at all. They've been encouraging me to bring you over for dinner. I talk about you so much that they're anxious to meet you."

"I'm looking forward to meeting them, too."

At 6:00 p.m. Charlie parked the blue Chevy in front of the house. As he and Jenny walked up the steps onto the porch, the front door was opened by his cherubic seven-year-old niece, Lauren.

"Hi, Uncle Charlie!" she chirped. "I've been looking out the window, watching for you!"

"We are a bit late. I hope that you didn't have dinner without us."

"No. Mommy got home late too. Supper isn't ready yet."

Charlie introduced Lauren to Jenny, then reached into the inner pocket of his jacket. "What's this in here?" he asked in pretend amazement. It was a ritual that he often went through for the amusement of the three Valentine children. "Why, it's a pack of wintergreen Lifesavers! The elves must have placed them in my pocket!"

Lauren giggled as Charlie gave her the candy. "Thanks, Uncle Charlie."

"And here are two more packs that the little fellows slipped into my pockets. Give those to your brother and sister."

"Okay. They're at the library. They should be home in a little while."

Violet came into the living room. "Hi, Charlie." She hugged Jenny. "It is wonderful to meet you."

"It is great to meet you, too. Thank you for inviting me to dinner."

"Well, I hope that both of you like what I prepared. The kids wanted to have spaghetti and meatballs for dinner."

"It's my favorite meal," Charlie said.

"But, Uncle Charlie, when you came to dinner last week, we had chili, and you said that was your favorite meal!" Lauren objected.

"Your mother is such a good cook that anything she prepares is my favorite meal."

"Charlie, when you made that trip to Ireland last year, you must have kissed the Blarney Stone," Gregory Valentine said as he entered the room.

"Alas, Blarney Castle wasn't on my itinerary," Charlie said.

"Your brother is simply an excellent judge of fine cuisine," Violet said.

"My tremendous powers of deduction tell me that this must be Jenny," Gregory said, shaking hands with her. "I suppose it doesn't take Sherlock Holmes to make that deduction."

Jenny laughed. "I think you have potential as a detective. We could use you on the police force."

"I'd better stay at the university," Gregory said. "My many mistakes cause less harm there."

Within a few minutes, everyone was seated at the table.

"So how go things at the university these days?" Charlie asked his brother.

"Pretty good. I just developed a new course that I'm going to be teaching every semester. It's based on the book **How the Catholic Church Built Western Civilization**. I want my students to understand that the Church played a key role in the development of law, literature, art, and architecture. Our modern legal system was patterned after canon law. The university was a gift from the Church to the world. The Church invented charitable work. In fact, the charitable spirit, as we know it in the Western world, was developed by the Church. The Church has always been the great defender of the sanctity of human life and also defending individual persons against the state."

"You are obviously very enthusiastic about that topic!" Charlie declared. "I hope that your students find your enthusiasm to be contagious."

"I have caught some of his enthusiasm," Violet said as she passed a bowl of mashed potatoes to Jenny. "I've borrowed a couple of his lesson plans to use with my high school science students."

" 'Borrowed' is a nice word for 'stolen,'" Gregory said with a grin.

"Oh, whatever!" she laughed. "In any case, I was intrigued to learn that the Church played such an important role in the development of science. Many great scientists like Louis Pasteur have been Catholic. Jesuit priests have especially made a great contribution. 35 craters on the moon are named after Jesuit scientists and mathematicians. And seismology, the study of earthquakes, is known as 'the Jesuit science' because it has been so dominated by Jesuits."

"It's funny that you mention the Jesuits," Jenny said. "Last week my father went over to the Jesuit Provincial Office and signed up for the Ignatian Volunteer Corps. He read about it in the *St. Louis Review*. Since he retired from the police force, he'd been getting a bit restless and was looking for some good cause for which he could do some charity work."

"What does the Ignatian Volunteer Corps do?" Violet asked.

"It mainly consists of retired men and women. They commit two days a week to serve the poor in St. Louis. Then, once a month, they meet for prayer and reflection about their service."

"It's wonderful that your father has found a way to keep active," Violet said. "I have read that elderly persons stay in better health if they find interesting activities in which to participate."

"Speaking of interesting activities," Gregory interjected. "Violet and I have four tickets for a play next week. **The**

Importance of Being Earnest by Oscar Wilde is playing at the Repertory Theatre in Webster Groves."

"I have always liked Oscar Wilde's plays," Jenny said. "He is a very good writer."

"Good," Violet said. "Gregory and I are hoping that you and Charlie can come with us to the play. It is a week from this Friday at eight o'clock. Are you both off-duty that evening?"

"We should be, unless something unexpected occurs," Charlie said. "We are involved with a heavy-duty case at the moment, but hopefully it will be resolved before next Friday."

"Thank you for the invitation," Jenny said. "I would love to go."

"Great," Gregory said. "We will be looking forward to spending the evening with the two of you."

"We will, too," Charlie said. "However, unfortunately, Jenny and I are going to have to cut our visit short this evening. We need to get to the airport to pick up two FBI agents. Their plane is scheduled to arrive in about an hour."

"Well, then I'm glad we will have more time together next Friday," Violet said.

After saying goodnight to the Valentine family, Charlie and Jenny strolled toward the car.

"I think that your brother and sister-in-law were trying to play the role of matchmakers for us," Jenny said, grinning at Charlie.

"I noticed that, too. Well, it is a night for romance." He pointed toward the night sky. "We have a full moon."

"Perhaps you'll turn into a werewolf," Jenny laughed.

"Let's hope not," Charlie said. "The moon certainly does have a lot of different meanings to different persons; priests, poets, philosophers, scientists, and storytellers --- the moon is an important image for all their mindsets."

Jenny reached over and gave him a hug. "You are certainly a smart cowboy."

Charlie eyebrows raised, pleasantly surprised; she had never previously hugged him. A short while ago, he had been amused by Gregory and Violet's matchmaking efforts. He had not thought that their efforts had any hope of succeeding. Now, however, as they got into the car, Charlie began to wonder whether someday he and Jenny might be more than partners on the police force.

CHAPTER 9

▼

A LITTLE RED DOT

Charlie and Jenny walked through Lambert Airport toward the passenger pick-up area where they would meet the two FBI agents. They glanced up at Charles Lindbergh's original personal monocoupe plane, which was on display, suspended above the lower level of the main terminal.

Because they were a few minutes early, they paused to look at one of the world's largest airport murals entitled "Aviation … An American Triumph." The 142-foot painting by Siegfried Reinhardt traced the history of flight.

The mural portrayed the ancient Greek myth showing the wings of Icarus melting when he flew too close to the sun, a giant 600-foot Chinese dragon kite, Leonardo da Vinci's aviation designs, hot air balloons, the Wright Brothers, Charles Lindbergh's flight from New York to Paris, and the space program.

"There's Neil Armstrong walking on the moon," Jenny pointed at the astronaut in the mural.

"Here's a pop quiz for you," Charlie said. "Who was the second man to walk on the moon?"

"Buzz Aldrin," Jenny replied without hesitation.

"Very good. I actually met Buzz Aldrin some years ago. While he was visiting a local bookstore, I shook hands with him and got his autograph."

"That's nice that you got to meet him." She squinted and looked at the mural very carefully. "Maybe Buzz Aldrin is in here somewhere. Every time I look at this mural, I see something that I never noticed previously," Jenny said.

"So do I," Charlie agreed. "That also happens to me at the New Cathedral. There are so many mosaics on the walls and ceiling that I always spot something new every time I go there."

"Did you know that there is a small Raggedy Andy mosaic included somewhere up there amidst all of the religious mosaics?"

"You're kidding?" Charlie asked in surprise.

"No, really."

"Among all of those mosaics of Jesus, the apostles, and saints, there is a mosaic of Raggedy Andy?"

"Yes, really."

"I recall that there are some pictures of modern saints like Katharine Drexel, Rose Philippine Duchesne, and Elizabeth Ann Seton in which they are depicted along with some orphans and other children that they taught. Is one of the children holding the doll?"

"I'm not telling, Charlie. You'll have to find the mosaic of the doll yourself the next time that you go there."

"And everyone tells me that I have such a nice partner." Charlie tried to glare at her, but he could not keep from laughing.

"No one tells me that about my partner," Jenny replied with a wide grin.

"Hey!" Charlie said with mock outrage, then glanced down at the time on his cell phone. "We'd better get over there to the gate. They will be here any second."

"We don't want to keep the FBI waiting."

Jenny and Charlie hurried over toward the passenger pick-up area and arrived just as two well-dressed men came through the gate. They introduced themselves to David Hummel and Sam Troutman.

"Is this your first time in St. Louis?" Jenny asked David.

"Yes. I grew up in Virginia. This is my first time here. I think that Sam was here once before. He's been everywhere."

"Not quite everywhere," Sam said. "However, I did make a brief visit to St. Louis about a year ago."

"So are you two the FBI terrorism experts?" Jenny inquired.

"I'm only an expert on cyber-terrorism," David said. "I was given this assignment because of my computer knowledge. I'm good with codes and databases. I can hack into almost any system. Sam is the expert on terrorists. He has been working in Europe and the Middle East for several years helping track down terrorists."

"Well, it sounds like the FBI sent the two right agents to St. Louis. I'm sure that you will be a big help."

"We will do our best," David promised.

"I'm anxious to speak with this Fatima Cedars," Sam said. "She sounds like she could be a goldmine of information."

"I think that she will be a valuable witness," Charlie said. "Fatima is also a very intelligent, pleasant person."

"I assume that you have her in a safe house?" Sam asked.

"Well, our police department budget is not sufficient for the department to have its own safe house for witnesses, so we needed to improvise a bit."

"We have Fatima in a house, and the house is safe; however, technically, it's not a safe house."

"Your riddle eludes me," Sam said.

Jenny laughed. "Fatima is staying at my father's house. No one besides us and our supervisor knows that she is there, so she should be safe. My father is a retired police sergeant, and he is capable of defending Fatima if the need arises."

"Your father's home should be adequate for tonight, but we will need to get her to a more secure local soon," Sam said. "David and I can check with the local FBI office to see what they have available."

"We're also anxious to speak with Dennis Sandhaven," David added. "His company's work on that Intelligent Agency project is vital to national security."

Charlie and Jenny accompanied the two FBI agents as they picked up their luggage, then drove the two agents to a downtown hotel near Union Station.

Walter was the first to notice the small red dot of light dancing with apparent innocence across the walls of the kitchen. Moving with a speed that belied his years, Walter jumped toward Fatima and dragged her to the floor.

"What's going on?" she exclaimed in astonishment.

"Stay down!" he cautioned. "Do you see that red light panning around the room? That is the laser sight of a gun."

"Oh, no!" Fatima declared.

As the dot moved closer to them, they heard glass break in the kitchen windows.

"He's firing a silenced weapon," Walter told her.

He reached up onto the counter and grabbed the phone. The hiss of two more muffled shots could be heard in the still night.

Walter did not hear any dial tone, but he tried dialing 9-1-1. The line was dead.

"Darn!" Walter dropped his phone. "He must have cut the phone line. It runs through the common ground into our backyard and then into the house."

"Don't you have a cell phone?" Fatima asked anxiously.

"Yes, but it's in the living room on a lamp table. He'd have too good a shot at us if we tried to get to it now. However, I can get to something else that will help us." Walter crawled cautiously along the floor, opened a draw in the kitchen counter, and pulled out his old service revolver.

"I'm so glad that you have a gun!"

"It might do the trick. If he decides to come charging in here, he'll be in for a big surprise."

"Where is he?"

"My best guess is that he has taken a firing position in the trees on the common ground. Judging by the location of his shots, he's moving around a bit to try to get a better angle."

"I think that I could make it to the light switch and turn it off," Fatima volunteered.

"No, even if you turned off that light, we'd still be silhouetted by the light coming in from the living room."

A bullet smashed into the wall about a foot over their heads, spraying some plaster onto them.

"He's moved into a better position. I was hoping to wait him out, but I'll have to take action before he gets us." Walter raised himself up onto one knee. "Stay down behind this counter, and I'll see if I can hit him. You'd better cover your ears, dear. My gun does not have a silencer."

As Fatima did so, Walker used the counter to brace his arm, estimating the best angle with which to return fire. In rapid succession, he fired six shots, changing the angle slightly with each shot in order to maximize his chances of hitting a target whom he could not see.

The explosion of gunfire resounded through the kitchen. Fatima was glad that she had taken his advice to cover her ears.

Walter lowered himself to a sitting position on the floor. He reloaded his gun.

"The little red dot is no longer panning around the kitchen," Fatima said. "You might have hit him, Walter."

"I was very lucky if I did. The odds are that I missed him. I certainly got his attention, though."

"Why isn't he still using his laser sight?"

"He's playing possum out there. He wants us to think that he went away or that he was hit by my shots. As soon as we stand up, he'd take us out."

"What can we do?"

"I'm going to give him another surprise." Walter crawled toward the back door.

"Be careful, Walter."

"Don't worry. Stay down."

He opened the door just wide enough for him to crawl outside. Walter left the door ajar in case he had to make a hasty retreat back into the house. Hoping that the shrubbery would keep him concealed, he slowly went forward.

The sniper could have anticipated this move that I'm making, Walter realized as he crept toward the corner of the house. At least I know this yard better than he does.

Walter peered around the corner toward the trees on the common ground beyond his property. He spotted the dark form of a man with a rifle positioned between a split tree trunk.

Walter crouched on one knee and took aim, steadying his gun arm with his other arm. It goes against my grain to shoot a man without shouting a warning, but in this case, I'll make an exception. I'm outgunned by a professional assassin; normal police procedure would get me killed here.

Just as Walter was about to fire, the laser scope on the assassin's rifle came on and the red beam swung toward Walter. He's seen me! In a moment of terror, Walter fired two quick rounds, then fell straight back and rolled against the house.

Mud was kicked up as bullets struck the spot where Walter had been a second earlier. Walter glanced back toward the kitchen door twenty feet away. He calculated that the sniper only needed to move about ten feet to get the angle for a clear shot at him.

Then Walter heard the sirens of police cars. They're still many blocks away, and I don't have time to get inside. Flattening himself on his stomach, he readied to fire from a prone position. He waited several breathless seconds, but the sniper did not appear.

A car door slammed, and an engine hastily started. Walter jumped up and hurried around the corner to see a car pulling away from the curb.

Although it was almost certainly the sniper's car, Walter couldn't be positive so he did not fire at it. By firing blindly through the kitchen window, he had taken a slight chance of hitting an innocent pedestrian. Now, he and Fatima were no longer in any immediate danger so there was no longer any justification for taking such a chance. It would have been a very long shot anyway.

Walter walked out to the front lawn to wait for the police. One of my neighbors must have heard the shots that I fired from the kitchen. If they hadn't called the police, I might be dead now.

Two police cruisers arrived almost simultaneously. As Walter went forward to speak with the uniformed officers, Fatima came out onto the front lawn. She rushed over to give Walter a hug.

Jenny and Charlie pulled up in his car. Jenny jumped out and ran up to her father.

"Dad! Are you all right?" She embraced him. "We heard the report of gunfire at this address, and Charlie got us here in record time. Apparently you've already taken care of matters."

"My aim could have been better," Walter said modestly. "He got away."

"Your father is far too humble," Fatima interjected. "He saved my life." She kissed Walter on the cheek. "He's my gallant hero."

Walter proceeded to describe everything that had happened. "I wish that I could have gotten a better look at the man, but it was too dark. I am certain that the shooter was a man. He looked like he was over six feet tall."

"Charlie and I can take a walk around the yard and common grounds in case he dropped something or left behind some other clue," Jenny said. "We should at least be able to find the shell casings."

Walter glanced at the broken windows. "There will be plenty of bullets in our kitchen for you to turn over to the evidence technicians."

"Dad, this has been a very stressful event," Jenny said. "Are you sure that you are all right? I'm worried about you."

"I'm fine, Jenny. I'm only 68 years old, and I'm in good shape for my age. I was a cop for my entire career, and I've been in many stressful situations through the years."

"Okay, I guess that I worry too much."

"We are going to have to move Fatima to a new location," Charlie said. "Do you think it will be safe for her to remain here for the rest of the night?"

"I'm off-duty now," Jenny said. "I can stay here with her and my father until morning. We can also post two officers outside in their cruiser."

"That should be enough to discourage our nemesis from making a return visit tonight," Charlie said. "Fatima, in the morning I'll stop by and take you to a new location where you'll be safer."

"Okay," Fatima said.

They all went into the kitchen to inspect the damage. A short while later, Charlie departed.

At about eight o'clock in the morning, he returned and dismissed the two officers who had maintained the vigil throughout the night.

Fatima was waiting inside with her travel bag packed. She profusely thanked Walter for his protection and hospitality, then she got into the car with Jenny and Charlie and rode away.

"In spite of what has happened, I am going to continue to work on the Intelligent Agency project. I won't allow the terrorists to stop me; I won't be intimidated. Since I have my laptop computer with me, I can do my work anywhere."

"Good," Jenny said. "You can help to get this Intelligent Agency project completed as soon as possible. Once that biotechnology program is running on numerous computers all over the United States, the extremists will have failed and no longer have any interest in you. You will be safe."

Fatima looked out the car window. "Where are you taking me?"

"To the Holiday Inn," Charlie said. "You, Jenny, and a policewoman will share a room there."

CHAPTER 10

▼

LOVELY LADY DRESSED IN BLUE

Later that evening, Jenny and Fatima went out onto the balcony of their hotel room.

Fatima held onto the balcony rail and gazed outward. "The moon is quite beautiful tonight."

Jenny smiled. "It's lovely. In fact, just last evening Charlie and I had dinner with his brother's family. As we were leaving, we both noticed the full moon and discussed the important symbolism of the moon. I know that the moon is an important symbol for the Islamic faith."

"Yes, it is."

"Fatima is a beautiful name."

"Thank you."

"I try to be an ecumenical person, so I like that your name has a connection to both the Christian and Muslim faiths."

"Yes, Mohammed's daughter was named Fatima. When she died, he wrote, 'Thou shalt be the most blessed of all the women in Paradise, after Mary.' I am also aware that there is a little village in Portugal named Fatima in which Mary appeared to some children in 1917. I once visited the Shrine of Our Lady of Lebanon near Beirut. Many Muslims visit that shrine."

"You are apparently an ecumenical person, too," Jenny said with a smile. "Mary has always been important to me." Jenny pointed toward the night sky. "In his sermon, I once heard a priest explain that the moon reflects the light of the sun and that is exactly what Mary does: she reflects the light of her Son. The priest quoted a great Christian scholar named Thomas Aquinas who said that 'As sailors are guided by a star to the port, so Christians are guided to Heaven by Mary.'"

"I am familiar with Thomas Aquinas," Fatima said.

"You certainly know about a lot of things in addition to computers and biotechnology. You have a broad spectrum of knowledge --- you're a Renaissance woman."

"And you know about many things besides your police work," Fatima said with a chuckle.

A few minutes later Charlie arrived, and he and Jenny took the elevator down to the lobby and went into the restaurant that was attached to the hotel lobby.

While they sipped their cappuccinos, Jenny told Charlie about her conversation with Fatima on the balcony.

"During my college days, I recall reading in a book by Fulton Sheen that in trying to spread the Christian faith, it is always best to start with that which people already accept."

"Like Saint Paul did that with the Romans," Jenny interjected. "Paul told the Romans that he had noticed their statue *To an Unknown God*. He proceeded to explain to them that this Unknown God was Jesus Christ."

"Exactly," Charlie said. "Modern missionaries can approach people in the same way as Saint Paul did. Since Muslims have a great admiration for Mary, our missionaries can expand and develop that esteem for her , knowing that Mary will carry the Muslims the rest of the way to Jesus Christ."

"Our Lady of Fatima can serve as the bridge that carries Muslims home to her Son," Jenny said.

CHAPTER 11

▼

EVERYTHING IS NOT AS IT SEEMS

"Your impatience has jeopardized this entire operation!" Saud Tariq glowered down at Elaine Sandhaven. She was a tall woman, but he was a very tall man.

"I had no choice!" she defended herself. "Do you understand? I had no choice. Dennis was getting suspicious of me. And he and his little Fatima were getting very close to completing that Intelligent Agency project. If I had not slowed them down, the United States government might now have that entire anti-biological warfare program."

"They would not have had the program. I had the situation under control. Now I need to clean up your mess. Why did you hire those two hit men, Marcus and Chuck? You had two Al Qaeda-trained operatives right here at this company. Shaukat Khan and Maulana Hafsa could have killed Dennis Sandhaven for you. It was not necessary to bring in outside help."

"Shaukat and Maulana have only worked here for two months. I only knew that they were sent to help with our biological warfare project. I thought that they were just computer nerds; I did not know that they were trained fighters."

Saud waved his hand dismissively. "What is done is done. I will try to correct the situation. Give me the names and all the information that you have about the two hit men that you hired."

"What are you going to do?"

"What do you think?" Saud asked contemptuously.

Elaine nodded. "I suppose they do have to die."

"Try not to create any more problems for me."

"You are being unjustly harsh with me. I have made a couple of mistakes recently, but overall I have done well and have served faithfully." Her eyes filled with tears. "I have sacrificed much for our cause. My husband has taken our son and disappeared. I might never see my son again!"

Saud's expression softened. "Perhaps I am taking out my frustrations on you. I am under a lot of pressure. The people who are pursuing me are not fools. I need to throw them off my trail."

Elaine had an idea. "Why don't we give the FBI a scapegoat? Perhaps then they will think they have got their man."

"Do you have someone in mind?"

"Yes. There is an Iranian here who would be the perfect scapegoat. He was once one of us, but he has become Americanized and no longer serves our cause."

Saud grinned at her. "You return to my good favor, sister."

CHAPTER 12

▼

QUID EST VERITAS?

Jenny and Charlie stopped by Ted Drewes Frozen Custard on Chippewa Street, then took their sundaes over to Francis Park, just a few blocks away. They parked, got out of the car, and sat on a park bench.

"When I was a teenager, I used to come over here to Francis Park sometimes to play tennis with a friend who went to Bishop DuBourg High School," Jenny said. "Of course, since I've always lived so close to Carondelet Park, that's usually been the park where I've done my bike riding and jogging."

"Almost every day over a thousand persons walk or jog around Francis Park," Charlie said as he scooped out another spoonful of frozen custard. "The park is a bit more than a mile around."

"Yes. The perfect distance for an evening walk."

"There's a church across the street from each of the four corners of the park." Charlie pointed down Nottingham Avenue at St. Gabriel the Archangel Church. "Sometimes this area is called 'Archangel Row.' Besides St. Gabriel's, you also have St. Raphael the Archangel parish here in St. Louis Hills and St. Michael the Archangel parish two miles away in Shrewsbury."

"I think that we might need some angelic help to catch this assassin," Jenny said. "He always seems to be one step ahead of us."

"You've noticed that, too. Do you have any ideas about how he is getting his information?"

"Maybe he's psychic," Jenny suggested jokingly.

Charlie laughed. "I'll believe that he is a psycho, but not a psychic. If he could read minds, he would have completed his mission by now and made his escape."

"I checked both of our cars for any electronic tracking device, but both cars were clean."

"I haven't washed my car in many weeks, Jenny. I certainly wouldn't say that it's clean."

"You know what I mean!"

"And we didn't discuss on the telephone where we sent Fatima Cedars, so it wouldn't matter if he was bugging the phone lines."

"See. He must be psychic."

"I'm afraid that he's getting inside information from someone either in our police department or in the FBI. Or the assassin could be a cop or FBI agent."

"You've discovered my secret identity as Jihad Jenny."

"I knew that you would confess sooner or later. However, Jihad Jenny, I don't think that you're the person that I'm looking for this week."

"Charlie, besides us, our supervisor is the only other person in the department who knew where Fatima was. I hardly think that Vincent Perkins is in league with an assassin."

"That would be hard to imagine. However, could he have written the information down somewhere and his note was found by the assassin or someone helping him?"

"Even that's pretty unlikely. I think that the weak link in the chain is with our FBI helpers."

"Really?" Jenny's eyebrows raised in surprise. "They both seem very smart."

"I don't doubt that they are smart. However, …"

Charlie was interrupted by the ringing of his cell phone. For his ringtone, he had a verse from an old country music song entitled *Beer for My Horses*. He liked both the tune as well as the law-and-order theme of the song.

Charlie glanced down at the caller ID on the phone. "Speaking of weak links who are smart," he said before flipping open the phone. "Hello, Sam. This is Charlie Valentine."

"Charlie, David and I have a lead on the identity of the killer. We'd like for you and your partner to join us when we go to his apartment to make the arrest."

A willowy woman in her mid-twenties with very curly brunette hair opened the door.

"Yes?" She was startled to see four persons at her door.

"Miss Jackie Avalon? My name is Jenny Halloran. I'm a detective with the St. Louis Police Department. This is Lieutenant Charlie Valentine." She held up her badge.

"I knew it. The second that I saw the four of you, I knew that you were cops."

"Actually, Lieutenant Valentine and I are the cops. These two gentlemen are FBI agents. May we come in?"

When she hesitated, Sam moved forward. "We have a search warrant. Lieutenant Halloran was just being polite." He was already in the doorway.

"Yes. Come in. What do you want?"

Sam squeezed past her into the apartment, carefully scanning the room.

"We have a few questions about Ali Aziz," Charlie said as they went into the living room. "I understand that he's a friend of yours."

"Yes. He lives here with me."

"He's your boyfriend?" David asked.

"Yes. For about a year. Why are you asking about him?"

Sam returned from a quick inspection of the kitchen. "Miss Avalon, last night the local FBI office received an anonymous phone call saying that Ali Aziz was working for an Islamic extremist group."

"No! No, he's not! He's just an art student at the university. We're both students there! That's where we met. He is an art student, not a terrorist. He hates violence."

"That would be the image that he projects to everyone," Sam said. "Do you know what a sleeper agent is?"

"No."

"A sleeper agent infiltrates a country and then becomes part of the society. He just leads a normal life for years before he receives a message to begin his subversive activities."

"Ali is not a sleeper agent or any type of agent," she insisted.

"Where is he right now?" Sam asked.

"He was at his job on campus, but he is due home any minute. Oh, this is all a mistake!"

"It might be," Jenny assured her. "Sometimes persons have come under unfair scrutiny."

Sam walked into the bedroom "Does your boyfriend have any weapons?"

"No!"

"Has he ever mentioned anything about a computer program called Intelligent Agency?" David inquired.

"No." She took her cell phone out of her purse. "I'd better call him. He might freak out if he walks in and sees the four of you."

"Put down that phone!" Sam commanded, coming out of the bedroom. "If you warn him, he'll run and you'll never see him again."

"I tell you that he's innocent!"

Sam held up some papers. "Then what were these doing on the desk? This is a newspaper article about Douglas Neldt's assassination. And here is a booklet about Islamic jihad."

"I have never seen those before," she objected. "We don't even subscribe to the newspaper." She again pulled her cell phone out of her purse. "I really should call him."

"I have told you that you can't," Sam said.

"You don't understand. It's important that he knows you're here so that he won't be startled when he arrives."

"Why?" David asked.

"It just is!"

"What aren't you telling us?" Sam demanded.

"He received a threatening phone call last night, and it freaked him out. He was afraid that someone might attack him today, so he took a gun with him to the campus."

"Damn!" David said.

"He's armed." Sam snapped open the buckle on his shoulder holster.

"Don't hurt him!"

"We won't," Charlie said. "We just want him to answer some questions."

"He might not be home for a while. After he gets off work, he often goes to the studio for an hour or so. Or he might stop by the deli."

"Does he have a permit for that gun?" David asked.

"I don't know."

"Why does he have a gun?"

"He had it packed away with some of his stuff. I think that he had almost forgotten that he owned a gun until he received that phone call last night."

"Why did he purchase the gun in the first place?"

She hesitated. "Years ago, when he first came to this country, he was involved with some Islamic extremists. I suppose that he could have been considered one of your so-called sleeper agents. But then he got to like life better in this country. He broke off all contact with the extremists. He likes America."

"At least that's what he told you," Sam said.

"It's the truth."

"The truth as you know it."

"Truth is truth."

"Veritas. Quid est veritas?" Sam asked.

Charlie went to the front window and looked outside. "So it might be a while until he gets home?"

"It's hard to say."

"While we're waiting, I'm going to take a quick look around the apartment," Charlie said.

"I'll join you in a few minutes," Jenny said, wanting to ask the woman some additional questions.

"Okay." Charlie went into the small kitchen and looked in the drawer and cabinets. Not finding anything of interest, he went into the one bedroom.

Charlie walked over to the computer on a small desk by the window. He considered turning it on, but he decided to wait until later because a thorough examination of the files could take a long time. He was especially interested in reading the man's e-mail.

Charlie searched the closet and found nothing unusual. He began going through a chest of drawers. Beneath a stack of tee-shirts, he found a knife.

"Jenny, could you come here a moment?"

She came into the room. "What do you have?"

He pointed at the knife, careful not to touch it. "Those look like bloodstains to me."

"I think you're correct." A tiny flashlight appeared in her hand, and she trained the beam on the blade of the knife.

"You have more gizmos than James Bond," Charlie said admiringly.

"A girl needs to be prepared," she said.

They heard the sounds of commotion coming from the living room. A woman was shouting.

Jenny and Charlie ran into the room to see the front door open. David was holding back Jackie, who was attempting to get to the door.

"Ali Aziz is out front!" David told the detectives, causing them to dash outside.

Sam was rapidly approaching the man. Ali Aziz shouted at him in Arabic, then pulled a handgun from his backpack and started to aim it at Sam.

With speed and efficiency, Sam drew his own weapon from his shoulder holster and shot Ali in the chest before the man could open fire.

Jenny was instantly on her cell phone calling for medical help. Having seen the shooting through the front window of her apartment, Jackie could no longer be restrained. She broke free from David's grip and ran outside down to the sidewalk, all the while screaming hysterically.

Her boyfriend was clearly dead. Charlie bent down and scooped up Ali's handgun so that Jackie could not do anything foolish. She knelt down and hugged Ali's body.

"Why? Why?" Her plaintive wail sounded up and down the street as neighbors emerged from apartments and houses.

Charlie said a silent prayer as he watched the woman cradling the body of her loved one in her lap. He had seen similar scenes through the years, and every time it reminded him of the Pieta, Michelangelo's great sculpture depicting Mary holding the body of Christ.

CHAPTER 13

▼

CURIOUSER AND CURIOUSER

Two hours later, Jenny and Charlie sat in a booth at the front window of a coffee shop in Webster Groves.

"It was a justifiable shooting." Jenny said. "We both saw what happened. I feel very sorry for Jackie, but Sam was defending himself."

"I don't like the way that entire incident transpired." Charlie took another sip of his cappuccino. "That man should not have died this afternoon."

"What do you mean?" Jenny asked.

"Both of us have gone to the homes of hundreds of suspects and arrested them without having to shoot them."

"But if Ali was the assassin, he was more dangerous than anyone that either of us has arrested."

"I doubt that he is the assassin. Did you see how he handled that gun? He was slow and clumsy. That guy at the counter who sold us these cappuccinos could probably have wielded that gun more efficiently."

"Very true," Jenny agreed.

For about a minute, they sat in companionable silence, enjoying their cappuccinos. It occurred to Jenny how comfortable she was in the presence of this man, her longtime partner and friend.

Charlie and my father are the two persons in this world with whom I am most comfortable, Jenny reflected. Does Charlie know how important he is to me? I can't imagine my life without him.

Then, out of the blue, she had a crystal clear vision of herself in a dazzling white wedding dress with Charlie at her side in a tuxedo. He had never looked more handsome.

Charlie looked at her intently. "Is something wrong?"

"Huh, oh, no, everything is fine." His question jolted her back to the present moment. "In fact, everything is perfect here."

"Everything is perfect here." Charlie looked at her warmly. "However, something is wrong with this case. Something is very wrong."

"Why do you say that?" Jenny asked.

"A minute ago I had an epiphany."

"Were you wearing a tuxedo?" she asked before she could stop herself.

"A tuxedo? What?" He looked bewildered.

"Never mind." Her face turned slightly red. "What was your epiphany?"

Charlie noticed her blush, but he decided to make no comment about it.

"How did those terrorists know that Fatima was at your father's house? We checked the cars; there was no electronic tracking device."

"Well, the only persons who knew where she was staying were David Hummel, Sam Troutman, you, me, my father, and our

Chief of Detectives, Captain Perkins. One of those persons could be an Al Qaeda operative. Who do you think it is?"

"I'm betting it's you," Charlie said dryly.

"Charlie!" Jenny laughed in mock outrage.

"Okay, then your father must be the Al Qaeda agent. Oh, wait, there was that whole gun battle thing. Al Qaeda shooting at Al Qaeda. That wouldn't work. As the biblical saying goes, 'A house divided against itself cannot stand.' I guess that clears Walter."

"Charlie, be serious."

"If I must, I will. Actually, I think there are more suspects available to us. Our two FBI associates might have told their own supervisor or some other FBI agent that Fatima was at your father's house. Or the terrorists might have intercepted one of our cell phone calls."

"We'll need to check with David and Sam about whether they told anyone."

"Let's just ask David first."

Jenny looked at him intently. "Why?"

"Even before he killed Ali Aziz, I had a bad feeling about Sam Troutman. There is something about that guy I don't like. This shooting just adds to my negative impression of him."

"Charlie, Sam Troutman is an FBI agent. Do you actually think that he could be helping Islamic terrorists? What would be his motive?"

"There are lots of possibilities," Charlie said. "Perhaps he is being forced to help them. Islamic extremists might be blackmailing him. Or terrorists might be holding one of his relatives hostage, either in this country or overseas."

"Or it could be pure, simple greed," Jenny added. "The terrorists might be paying him for information."

"Right. Besides, it is not unheard of for an FBI agent to go bad. Back in the 1990s, there was an FBI agent who was selling top-secret information to the Russians."

"Okay, let's contact David." Jenny took out her cell phone. "I have his number in my list of contacts." She made the call, then waited for several seconds. Just when she thought that she was going to have to leave a message on voice mail, he answered.

"Hello, Lieutenant Halloran."

"Hello, Agent Hummel. What's new?"

"Not much. I'm troubled about that shooting earlier today."

"Actually my partner and I have been discussing the shooting, and we have some concerns that we'd like to discuss with you," Jenny said.

"Do you want me to bring Sam with me?" David asked.

"No. We'd like to speak with you alone. In fact, it would be better if you didn't even tell Sam that you are meeting with us."

"I understand. Where would you like to meet?"

"Charlie and I can come to your location. Where are you?"

"When you called, I was just pulling into the parking lot of a Steak and Shake on South Lindbergh Boulevard. I was planning to go inside, but I can eat later."

"No, go ahead and get something to eat there. I know exactly where that Steak and Shake is. There's a Walgreens next door. Charlie and I are just a few miles from where you are. We can be there in about ten minutes."

"Okay, I'll see you then."

"Bye." Jenny hung up. "He just arrived at the Steak and Shake on Lindbergh Boulevard near Tesson Ferry Road."

Charlie stood up. "Good, let's go."

"Curiouser and curiouser," she said as they walked toward their car. "That Alice was a smart young lady. Life is filled with curious things."

"What?" Charlie looked at her.

"I was quoting from **Alice in Wonderland**," Jenny said. "The complete sentence is 'Curiouser and curiouser!' cried Alice (she was so much surprised that, for the moment, she quite forgot how to speak good English).'"

"What?"

"We seem to be saying 'what' a lot lately," Jenny remarked.

"What are we saying a lot lately?"

"What."

"What are we saying a lot lately?" Charlie repeated.

"The word 'what!'" she declared.

"Who's on first?" he said with a grin.

"Charlie, you're going to get it!" Jenny realized that he had understood all along; he had merely been playing a variation of an old comedy routine.

"Getting back to the subject at hand, you mentioned that you found something to be curious. What was curious?"

"David did not ask why we wanted to meet with him without Sam and not tell Sam about the meeting."

"David probably assumes that we are more comfortable discussing the shooting without Sam being present," Charlie said as they got into his blue Chevy.

"I suppose so." Jenny got into the car, and they drove away.

About ten minutes later they pulled into the parking lot of the Steak and Shake restaurant.

When they entered the restaurant, they immediately spotted David, who was seated comfortably in a booth in the far corner.

"I always like to sit with my back against the wall," he told them jokingly as they slid into the booth with him. "It makes it impossible for my enemies to sneak up behind me."

"This is your first visit to St. Louis," Charlie said with a smile. "You can't have made too many enemies here."

"You might be surprised."

"Jenny and I have been cops for years. We have a whole busload of enemies here. We are the ones who need the corner seats."

"I have your back. Don't worry."

A waitress approached their table and gave menus to Charlie and Jenny.

"This lovely young lady is Ana," David introduced her. "She was also my waitress yesterday, and we had a nice conversation. Ana mentioned that she is a vegetarian, so I told her that I would be an honorary vegetarian for the day. I'm having a grilled cheese sandwich."

"Actually a grilled cheese sandwich sounds good to me," Charlie said. "I'll also be a vegetarian for the day. I would also like a vanilla shake."

"A vegetarian waitress at Steak and Shake," Jenny remarked. "That's rather ironic." She glanced at the waitress's name tag. "And you spell 'Ana' with one 'n.' I don't think that I have seen that previously."

Ana laughed. "Well, my actual name is spelled 'Anna,' but I prefer to spell it with one 'n.' I suppose that I like to be unique."

After Ana departed to get their food, the two police detectives and the FBI agent lowered their voices.

"While we were speaking on the phone a little while ago, I had the impression that you share some of our concerns about Sam," Jenny said.

"I have always considered the guy to be very overrated. He is supposed to be one of our best experts on the jihadist movement, yet almost every operation with which he has been involved has failed. When he was stationed in Europe, he participated in several raids against terrorist groups, but something always went wrong, and someone besides Sam got the blame for the failure. A few months ago his team raided a pub in Berlin, but they were ambushed and several German intelligence officers were killed by the terrorists, who then escaped. In five major raids led by Sam, only a few low-level operatives were arrested or killed."

"Sacrificial lambs," Charlie said, deep in thought.

"Sam also unsuccessfully led the FBI's pursuit of an assassin named Saud Tariq. Tariq murdered numerous moderate Islamic leaders in Arab countries and in Europe."

"Why was the FBI involved?"

"Saud Tariq killed a CIA agent in London. The CIA agent had infiltrated an extremist group, but somehow his cover was blown. He was stabbed to death when he entered his apartment in the Soho district in London."

"That sounds familiar," Jenny said. "That computer programmer, Rebecca Wright, was stabbed to death when she entered her apartment."

"It's possible that Saud Tariq killed her," David said. "We think that he assassinated Douglas Neldt and arranged for his company to be bombed."

"Why are we just hearing about Saud Tariq now?" Charlie asked.

"Sam did not want me to mention him to you. We weren't sure that Saud Tariq was involved, and Sam said that he didn't want to tell you about him until we had more facts. He is big on the concept of need to know. He said that he doesn't believe Saud Tariq is in St. Louis, so there is no need for St. Louis police to know about him. We aren't even sure that Saud Tariq is in the United States."

"But you think that he is here?" Jenny inquired.

"I would bet a year's salary that he is. You two are lucky to have each other as partners. Working with Sam is a pain in the neck. To tell you the truth, Sam doesn't have much respect for the police. He can be a snob sometimes. Sam hasn't said anything negative about either of you, though." He grinned slightly. "In fact, you're the first police detectives that he hasn't made snide remarks about to me. So, in a way, that's kind of an indirect compliment to you."

"Be still my heart," Jenny said with a sardonic grin.

Ana arrived with the shakes and plates of food.

"Just before you arrived, Ana was telling me about her high school graduation," David said. "She went barefoot beneath her gown."

"Yes," Ana said with a smile. "I didn't think anyone noticed that I was barefoot, but my grandmother asked me about it after the ceremony. Apparently when I came down the steps from the stage, she noticed my feet."

"The barefoot graduate," Jenny laughed. "That is hilarious, Ana!"

"Where are you going to college, Ana?" David asked.

"I'm going to Loyola University in New Orleans. Last year I went with my sister, Linden, to visit both Loyola University of Chicago and Loyola University in New Orleans. Both schools looked good, but I like the nice warm weather down south."

"Oh, that should be great, Ana," Jenny said. "New Orleans is a fascinating place."

"And it is warm enough for you to go barefoot there," Charlie grinned.

"Exactly," Ana chucked. "I can't wait to start school there. But I will be back working here during Christmas break and summer vacation."

"Good," Charlie said. "We will stop by here at Christmastime to hear about how college is going for you."

Ana spotted some new customers entering the restaurant, so she excused herself and went to greet them.

Jenny glanced over at Charlie, who was looking out the window at the parking lot, apparently lost in thought. "Earth to Charlie. Come in, Charlie."

"I'm listening."

"Yes, but are you listening to us or to some inner voice telling you to kill the bad people at the table with you?"

Charlie laughed. "Fortunately for you and David, I'm ignoring that inner voice."

She looked over his shoulder. "So what are you thinking?"

"I was thinking about Ana going barefoot beneath her gown at graduation," Charlie said.

"Are you considering going barefoot, too, Charlie?" Jenny kidded him. "I think our Chief of Detectives would frown upon that. He is not even real thrilled about you wearing those cowboy boots all the time."

"No, I won't be going barefoot; I like my boots," Charlie said. "However, the point is that human beings are curious creatures who do surprising things."

"So?"

"So I'll bet that Sam Troutman has done a lot of surprising things."

"Why?" David asked.

"Because we have been worried about how the terrorists found out that Fatima was staying with Jenny's father. Only the police and FBI knew where she was staying, and we know that our side was secure. Did you mention her safe-house location to your supervisor or to any other FBI agent?"

"No. I didn't tell anyone. And Sam wouldn't have had any good reason to tell anyone."

"His reasons might not have been good," Charlie said. "This security breach, the unnecessary shooting death earlier today, and what you have told us about Sam's record in other countries makes me very suspicious of him."

David nodded. "I agree."

"A short while ago, Jenny and I were discussing the possibility that Sam is being paid by Al Qaeda to give them information. Or he might be being blackmailed by Al Qaeda or threatened by Al

Qaeda. They could be threatening his family or holding someone hostage to get him to cooperate."

David shook his head. "I doubt it. I have known the guy for over a year. He acts the same now as he did a year ago. He seems just as relaxed as usual." He paused. "Even killing that guy earlier today did not seem to bother him. That seemed strange to me. Less than an hour after the shooting, he was looking for a good restaurant in which to eat lunch."

Charlie looked at him intently. "I just had an idea. It might be kind of crazy, but it is worth investigating. Could you have the FBI send a list of Sam's assignments in Europe and the Middle East? I would also like the FBI to send a list of the places and dates of all the known hits by Saud Tariq in Europe and the Middle East."

David's eyes widened. "What are you implying?"

"Nothing yet. I just want those two lists so that I can compare the movements of Sam Troutman and Saud Tariq."

At that moment, Ana arrived with the bill, which she placed on the table. She had noticed that they were almost finished with their sandwiches and shakes. "ST and ST," she said as she set down the bill.

"Thanks," David said, taking a sip from his chocolate shake. "What do you mean, ST and ST?"

She laughed. "Oh, I just heard you say those two names. They have the same initials. I guess that is not very unusual, though."

A look of smoldering fury appeared on David's face. Noticing his change in expression, Ana hurriedly added, "Did I say something wrong?"

"No, Ana," he quickly reassured her. "You are wonderful. I am angry with myself for overlooking the obvious. I am even more angry with an arrogant fiend who has been playing us for fools. He is soon going to find out who the real fool is."

"Keep cool, David," Jenny told him. "We don't know anything for certain at this point. We need to compare those two lists."

"Yes, but I know in my bones what the result is going to be."

"I agree," Charlie said. "The truth has been right there in front of us."

After paying the bill and saying goodbye to Ana, the two detectives and the FBI agent went out onto the parking lot.

"This might take a while," David said. "Getting the Saud Tariq information should be easy, but getting the information about Sam will be more complicated. I might have to call in one or two favors that are owed to me."

"Charlie and I are heading to police headquarters downtown," Jenny said. "Please let us know as soon as you get those two lists."

"Right. I will try to get them to you as soon as possible."

As Jenny and Charlie drove away, David made a call on his cell phone. "Hi, this is David. We have a problem."

CHAPTER 14

▼

TREACHERY

Charlie and Jenny drove east on Lindbergh Boulevard to Highway 55, which they then took north to downtown St. Louis. Sunset was approaching, and Jenny looked out the car window as twilight enhanced the beauty of the Gateway Arch and the Old Cathedral on the Mississippi riverfront.

Jenny had always found downtown interesting; she liked the combination of old, historic buildings sharing the same city blocks with gleaming, new skyscrapers. The best of the old and the best of the new, "The Best of Both Worlds," Jenny smiled as she recalled a popular Hannah Montana song from a few years ago.

When Jenny was a child, her father had occasionally brought her down to police headquarters, which were next door to city hall. The police officers and office staff always treated her like a little princess, so she always enjoyed her visits. She believed that these early positive experiences influenced her decision to follow her father into police work.

After going into the police headquarters building, Charlie went into Captain Vincent Perkins office in order to give an update to their supervisor. Meanwhile, Jenny went over to her desk in order to check the memos in her inbox.

"How is your father doing, dear?" Barbara Spencer asked Jenny. Barbara was a longtime secretary with the police department; she was approaching retirement age and had worked with Walter Halloran for ten years.

"He's doing fine, Barb. I think that he liked all the excitement."

"Well, he should be proud of himself for doing such a marvelous job defending that young woman. He was always an excellent police officer."

"Thank you. I'll tell him that you said so."

Charlie emerged from Captain Perkins's office and approached her. Jenny looked at him quizzically.

"How did it go?"

"Captain Perkins said that you and I are outstanding human beings and should be commended for our fine detective work."

"So how did it really go?"

"He thinks that we are insane to suspect that an FBI agent is an Al Qaeda assassin. He said that if he gets any complaints about us from FBI officials, he might pull us off this case."

"That sounds more like the Captain Perkins that we know and love," Jenny said.

Charlie's cell phone rang, and he glanced at the caller ID. "It's David."

"Let's hope he has some information for us."

Charlie flipped open the phone. "Hi, David."

"Charlie, I have the lists!" Charlie could clearly hear the excitement in the agent's voice.

"That's great, David. That was fast work."

"Getting the Saud Tariq list was easy. I mean it was easy to get the FBI records office to send me all of the information that they had about Saud Tariq. We don't have a complete itinerary of all of his movements; there are weeks and even months when we have no idea where Saud Tariq was."

"As you know, my guess is wherever Sam Troutman was, Saud Tariq was. A man doesn't wander far from his shadow."

"You're right. At least I'm pretty sure that you are right. Getting the Sam Troutman list was more difficult since he is an active agent in good standing. I did need to call in a favor, but it paid off big-time."

"How so?"

"There is a perfect overlap of some of the cities and dates on the two lists. Sam was in London the same week that Saud Tariq shot a moderate Islamic leader in London who encouraged peaceful coexistence with the West. Sam was in Berlin the same week that Saud Tariq killed an informant in Berlin who had been providing information to German intelligence about jihadists in that country. Sam was in Paris the same week that a sniper shot a counter-intelligence officer. The French police believe that Saud Tariq was the sniper."

"Good work, David." Charlie flashed a two thumbs-up sign to Jenny.

"I have both the lists downloaded onto my cell phone," David said. "I can email the lists to you and your partner."

"That would be great. Thanks."

"Okay, hold on. I'm sending the lists now."

A few seconds later the cell phones of both Charlie and Jenny signaled that they had received messages. The two detectives eagerly scanned the documents that David sent.

"Bingo!" Jenny declared. "It's true. Sam Troutman is Saud Tariq. I can't believe it!"

"We are going to take Sam into custody as soon as possible," David said. "I'm on my way downtown now. I will meet you outside the local FBI office. We can get an arrest warrant and then take Sam into custody."

After saying goodbye to David, Charlie and Jenny briefly stopped by their supervisor's office in order to give him the latest information and show him the lists on their phones. They were both amused by the look of astonishment on Captain Vincent Perkins's face. Although the man could sometimes be difficult, Jenny and Charlie both liked him and had a good relationship with him.

Captain Perkins grudgingly complimented them on their correct deductions. He stood in the doorway of his office and watched as they departed. Those are the two best detectives in the St. Louis Police Department, he reflected. Even before today, I thought so. I have never heard anyone say anything negative about either of them, and they solve almost every single case to which they were assigned.

In a million years, I would never tell them how much respect I have for them. I'm probably kidding myself. They probably already know how much I respect them. They figure everything else out -- at least almost everything else. Their own relationship is their only unsolved mystery.

All of the detectives, including myself, and the office staff are sure that those two will marry someday. They seem almost destined to be married to each other, but they don't seem to realize that yet. Oh, well, I'm sure they will also figure that out eventually. Captain Perkins grinned and went back into his office.

While he was relaxing in his downtown hotel room, Sam Troutman's cell phone rang. He did not recognize the caller ID.

"Yes? Troutman here," he answered.

"Agent Troutman. This is Franklin Kincell from the Bureau's data processing division. I assisted you with obtaining some information a few months ago."

"Oh, yes, Franklin, I remember." Sam recalled bribing the man in order to get unauthorized access to information about the FBI's overseas intelligence sources. The information had been well worth the money that he paid Franklin. Several of those overseas intelligence sources were now dead.

"Good, I'm glad that you remember me," Franklin resumed. "The reason that I am calling is that, when I helped you with that other matter, you asked me to let you know whenever someone electronically accessed your personnel records."

Sam's body tensed. "And someone did so?"

"Yes. I set things up so that I would receive an instant message if your personnel record was accessed. About ten minutes ago our data processing department accessed both your personnel records and the case records of an Al Qaeda agent named Saud Tariq."

Damn! Sam closed his eyes and struggled to control his emotions. "To whom did they send those records?" he asked in a carefully-modulated voice.

"To Agent David Hummel."

Sam maintained his control and asked, "Only to David Hummel?"

"Yes. The request for the information was sent by him as urgent and high-priority. I doubt that the data processing department staff even took the time to read over the records that they sent. However, I did, and it was very interesting. I compared the lists of where you have been with the list of the Saud Tariq's activities. The comparison was fascinating."

"I was pursuing Saud Tariq for quite some time," Sam said.

"Okay, let's go with that explanation. However, I still think that my information this evening is worth a lot more money than I received previously --- a lot more."

"How much?"

"A hundred thousand dollars should be sufficient."

"I will have that amount electronically transferred into your bank account. You have done well. I assume that I can count on your silence."

"Of course, as long as I receive my money. However, if I'm not paid in the next day or two, I'll have to have a conversation with some FBI officials."

"You will receive your money," Sam said tersely. "Now forward to my cell phone the same records that were sent to David Hummel."

"I will send the records to you immediately."

"That will be fine. I'm glad that you called. Goodbye."

"Bye."

I can't believe that little twerp in trying to blackmail me, Sam thought incredulously. I was going to have to kill him anyway; he knows too much. However, blackmailing me absolutely necessitates that I kill him. His greed overcomes his common sense. Blackmailing an assassin --- not a good idea, Sam thought with a wry smile.

Others will have to die, too. I need to contain this breach so that I can continue to work for the FBI. David Hummel has probably told those two police detectives about what he has learned; all three will have to die.

He closed his briefcase in which the parts to his telescopic rifle were concealed behind a special lining. Sam carried the briefcase with him as he left the hotel room and headed for the elevator down to the lobby.

I know where David will be going, he reflected, and I need to stop him before he gets there. It is too bad that I have to kill him;

on a personal level, I like the guy. The two police detectives are also amiable. I will also need to kill Fatima Cedars and Dennis Sandhaven. Unfortunately, this will be a very bloody week.

So it must be. In jihad, we do what must be done.

CHAPTER 15

▼

BATTLE ON HIGH

Meanwhile, Jenny and Charlie emerged from the building and headed toward the car.

"Actually we could just walk over to the FBI offices," Jenny said. "It's just a few blocks."

"It's five long blocks," Charlie said. "Although I could use the exercise, we need to resolve this situation swiftly. God only knows what Sam Troutman is doing right now."

"Okay. You win. We'll drive there."

"You certainly didn't need much persuading," Charlie laughed.

"Well, you're right about the importance of saving time."

They drove five blocks west and parked on Market Street near the Milles Fountain, an elaborate fountain display called the "Wedding of the Waters," symbolizing the Mississippi and Missouri Rivers, which merged a short distance north of the city.

It was almost completely dark as they crossed Market Street and walked alongside Union Station. The huge, Romanesque-style train station had been transformed into a shopping, restaurant, and hotel complex.

A few months earlier, Charlie had purchased his nieces and nephew a train set from the miniature railroad store in Union Station. Shortly before Christmas, Gregory, Violet, and the children had set up the train tracks around the base of the Christmas tree. While he ate Christmas dinner with them, Charlie had enjoyed watching his gift in motion as the train circled the tree.

On this evening, though, his thoughts remained focused on their mission. The local FBI offices were located in a building just west of Union Station. As they crossed the driveway and approached the lobby of the building, David Hummel and a tall, distinguished-looking man came out the front entrance.

"Oh, perfect timing," David said as he spotted Jenny and Charlie. "Robert, these are the two detectives that I told you about. This is Lieutenant Charles Valentine and his partner, Lieutenant Jennifer Halloran." He looked at them. "Detectives, this is Robert Webber, the assistant director of operations for this region."

Charlie and Jenny shook hands with the FBI official.

"David tells me that the two of you are primarily responsible for cracking this case," Webber told them. "Thank you for your help."

"We are glad to be of service," Jenny said.

"This is certainly a shocking situation," Webber continued. "I can't believe that we have another rogue agent. And this one is a killer!"

"Three agents are going to meet us at the hotel," David said. "Hopefully we can take Sam by surprise there."

"He is a very dangerous man," Webber said.

As they walked toward David's rental car, two gunshots rang out. Charlie and Jenny instantly had their pistols in their hands, and David was only a fraction of a second slower than the two police detectives.

Robert Webber, though, collapsed to the pavement, having been hit by both of the shots.

"We're too much in the open here!" Jenny shouted as she and Charlie looked for the shooter. "Let's get him behind that car!"

As David, Charlie, and Jenny dragged Webber behind a Monte Carlo, two more gunshots shattered the windows of the car.

"The sniper is firing from the rooftop of that building across the street!" Charlie exclaimed.

"Robert is dead," David said sadly, looking up from the body of the FBI official.

"I'm very sorry, David," Jenny said and added a silent prayer for Webber's soul.

"Is Sam the sniper?" David asked.

"I can't tell from this distance," Charlie said. "At the moment he would have a hard time hitting us, but he is moving on that rooftop to a better angle from which he can hit us. We are going to have to get over toward that stairwell."

"We will be in the open for several seconds if we try to get there," David said.

"That's the only option," Charlie said, rising from his crouching position. "We will need to leave Robert's body here for now. I will provide cover fire as we run toward the stairwell. Okay, let's move! Now!"

With all three running at top speed, Charlie kept himself between the sniper and Jenny while he fired several shots toward the shadowy figure on the rooftop across the street. Charlie could see the sniper duck for cover, seemingly surprised by the return fire. He did not get any shots at the trio before they reached the temporary safety of the stairwell.

"We should wait here for help to arrive," David told Charlie while Jenny used her cell phone to call for back-up help from other police officers.

"We can't," Charlie said, pointing across the street. "Can you see him up there? He is already moving to a different spot from where he can hit us here."

David squinted as he attempted to discern the identity of the sniper. "I'm fairly sure that is Sam! Damn him to hell!"

Charlie snapped a new clip into his pistol. "I might be able to get him," he said with more conviction that he felt.

"I have a whole army of police on the way, Charlie," Jenny said as she ended her cell phone call.

"We don't have time to wait for them. You and David should stay here. Stay crouched down against the steps. These glass walls give him a clear view into the stairwell, but it is getting dark, and he might not spot you right away. And I'm planning on keeping him busy."

"Be careful, Charlie!" Jenny implored him.

"I will," he promised as he as ascended.

Charlie went up the stairwell as high as he could; the stairwell did not go all the way up to the roof. He exited outside onto a mezzanine level, remaining crouched as he moved rapidly across the mezzanine.

For a brief time, Charlie thought that the sniper was unaware that he had ascended to that level. However, that idea was quickly dispelled when two shots smashed into the air conditioning unit only three feet away from Charlie.

The loud hum of the air conditioning unit instantly stopped, replaced by the hiss of escaping freon. The hissing sound reminded Charlie of the hiss of a viper.

His survival instincts prompted Charlie to keep moving. It occurred to him that the sniper was not very good at hitting moving targets. He probably has never had much practice shooting at a moving target, Charlie deduced, as he bobbed and wove amongst the cornices and buttresses.

Charlie went up a small ladder to reach the ledge directly below the roof from which protruded a communications tower. As Charlie crawled on his stomach along the ledge, he noticed the elaborate stonework that decorated the Market Street side of the building.

A dozen griffins lined that entire side of the ledge. The griffin was a mythical creature with a lion's body and an eagle's head and wings, often symbolizing Christ's majestic power over both land and sky. Charlie recalled that the griffin sometimes served as a symbolic defender of the Church. I hope that these griffins can defend me this evening, he thought as he paused to catch his breath.

Wondering why the sniper had not shot at him for almost a minute, Charlie peeked out from behind one of the griffins. That is definitely Sam, he realized with some sadness as he got a clear view of the man with the rifle on the ledge of the building on the north side of Market Street.

Charlie noticed that the ledge upon which Sam stood was lined by a number of gargoyles, hellish creatures that seemed to stare defiantly at the griffins directly across the street. I wonder whether the architects planned it that way, Charlie speculated. Well, at least Sam is amongst friends.

As he supported himself against a griffin, Charlie was able to get some surreptitious looks at Sam. He noticed that Sam's head was tilted slightly upward. He thinks that I moved up to the roof since it is the highest level, Charlie realized. That is what he would have done if he had been in my position. That probably would have been the smart thing to do. That would give me a better angle from which I could shoot down at him.

It certainly would have been smart of me to have gone up there. However, now it would be too dangerous to try to get up there. Let's see if I can turn my misstep to my advantage.

Five seconds later, Charlie saw his opportunity. While remaining behind the gargoyle, Sam stood up in order to get a better view.

Charlie sprang up with his gun aimed directly at Sam, who saw him just a fraction of a second before Charlie fired three shots. Two of the bullets shattered the gargoyle's head, its hideous visage crumbling into fragments and dust. The third bullet flew through the empty space where Sam had been an instant earlier. Sam's lightning-fast reflexes had kept him alive.

Sirens from numerous police cars grew steadily louder. I need to leave now or I will be captured, Sam realized. Besides there is no longer any reason to kill this detective, his partner, or my own partner. My cover is blown, and my career in the FBI is over. Sam Troutman is no more; from this moment on, I am Saud Tariq and jihad is my life.

I will leave this country in the morning. However, I still need to kill Fatima and Dennis Sandhaven in order to try to stop the Intelligent Agency program. Our scientists in our secret laboratory have almost perfected a doomsday virus, but the virus will be worthless if Intelligent Agency is activated; Intelligent Agency can easily defeat our doomsday virus. I must stop Intelligent Agency.

With nightfall complete, Saud Tariq descended down the dark stairwell and vanished like a phantom.

While Saud Tariq made his escape, Charlie cautiously moved into the open, keeping his gun trained across the divide that had separated him from his foe. Charlie knew that Sam could have feigned a retreat in order to draw Charlie out into the open.

When he was convinced that Sam was actually gone, Charlie headed down toward Jenny, David, and the numerous police officers who were beginning to swarm up both buildings and all over the surrounding city blocks.

"Charlie!" Jenny ran into his arms. "I was so afraid that you had been killed!"

"I'm a bit surprised that I am still alive. I was overmatched both in firepower and in skill." As he withdrew from her hug, he looked at David. "The sniper was Sam Troutman. I got a clear look at him."

David shook his head. "Unbelievable. Sam killed Robert Webber. This is like a nightmare." He pulled out his cell phone. "I need to make a couple of calls. With all these sirens wailing, I won't be able to hear out here, so I'm going back inside." David went into the office building in which the FBI offices were located.

Charlie and Jenny conferred with other detectives and police officers who had arrived, anxious to hear their account of the sniper attack.

About twenty minutes later, David emerged from the office building and approached them. "The big shots are on the way here," he declared. "Some FBI officials and the top government computer experts are taking redeye flights to St. Louis tonight."

"Why?" Jenny asked.

"They want to get that Intelligent Agency program running as soon as possible. The computer experts want to meet with Fatima and Dennis Sandhaven tomorrow morning."

"That's fast work," Jenny said.

"Yes. And, with some luck, Intelligent Agency will be up and running by tomorrow afternoon. The anti-viral, anti-biological warfare program will be safe then because it will be stored on dozens of mainframe computers all around the United States. Sam and the other terrorists won't be able to stop it."

"Great," Charlie said.

"Speaking of Fatima and Dennis, where are they?" David asked.

"They are staying in two rooms at the Holiday Inn on Hampton Avenue. Sergeant Mitch O'Brien and two other police officers are protecting them."

"Good. When the computer experts arrive in the morning, I will have them brought directly to that hotel. We can set up a temporary computer lab in one of the hotel's conference room and get Intelligent Agency activated."

Charlie glanced at the time on his cell phone. "Jenny, you and I need to get over to the Holiday Inn. We are scheduled to be the overnight bodyguards."

"Charlie, you were almost killed about a half hour ago!" Jenny exclaimed. "You should go home and get a good night's sleep. We can get another cop to take over your guard duty tonight."

"I'm irreplaceable, my dear," Charlie said, grinning wryly. "Haven't you figured that out by now?"

"Actually I have," Jenny laughed.

Meanwhile, about a mile away, Saud Tariq had successfully slipped past the small army of police that had converged near Union Station. After boarding a Metrolink train heading west toward Shrewsbury Station, Saud sat down, took out his cell phone, and made a call.

"Hello, Agent Troutman," Franklin Kincell answered. "I'm surprised to hear from you tonight."

"Yes, well, I'm surprised to be calling you. Listen, I don't have much time."

"No, I don't suppose so," Kincell chortled. "You've gotten yourself into a very difficult situation."

"You already know about that?"

"I try to keep on top of things. I'm sorry that the information that I provided didn't help you more. However, I do still expect to be paid."

"You'll get your money, but I need some additional information. I need you to find out where Fatima and Dennis Sandhaven are staying."

"It might be possible for me to obtain that information for you. Unfortunately, due to your present situation, I must insist on immediate payment. I want an additional one hundred thousand dollars. And you still owe me a hundred thousand dollars for the information that I sent you earlier this evening."

Damn this miserable little toad, Saud thought silently. I wish that I could kill him myself, but I need to get out of America tomorrow, so one of my brothers will have the pleasure of squashing this toad.

"Agent Troutman? Are you still there?"

"Yes, Franklin. The money will not be a problem. I will have the money electronically transferred into your bank account right now. I'll call you in a few minutes after I complete the transaction."

"Good. And, while you are doing that, I will begin searching for the information that you need."

"All right. I'll speak with you shortly."

Using his cell phone, it took Saud about ten minutes to transfer two hundred thousand dollars into Franklin's bank account. He wondered whether there would be some way to retrieve the money after Franklin's death later this week.

After completing the transfer, he called Franklin, who then requested some additional time in order to verify that the money transfer had been successful and to complete his research.

While Saud waited an additional fifteen minutes, he became impatient and was about to call Franklin again when his cell phone rang.

"Agent Troutman, I've verified that the money has been transferred into my account. And you will be glad to hear that I found out where they are staying. I intercepted a text message that Agent David Hummel sent to your FBI superiors and to several computer experts with the NSA, the National Security Agency."

"Thank you," he said sarcastically. "I was aware what the NSA acronym stood for. Where are they staying?"

"At a Holiday Inn on Hampton Ave at Wilson Street. It is near Highway 44."

Saud smiled. This little toad named Franklin is good at what he does. I hope that his honor was worth the money that I sent him.

"Do you have a room number at the hotel?"

"No."

"The room number does not matter. The information that you gave me will be sufficient. You have done well." Saud surprised himself by adding that compliment at the end.

"Thanks. Well, I guess that you will be leaving the FBI, but you know how to reach me. It has been a pleasure doing business with you, Agent Troutman."

"Thank you, good night."

After completing his call with Franklin, Saud called Maulana Hafsa, Shaukat Khan, and Sharif Saffa. To each of these three persons, he gave the same message: meet me in the parking lot of the Shrewsbury Metrolink Station as soon as possible. Bring all of your weapons. It is a night for jihad.

CHAPTER 16

▼

DOUBLE JEOPARDY

Jenny and Charlie parked on the lot of the Holiday Inn on the east side of Hampton Avenue. There was a Drury Inn on the west side of the street and a Red Roof Inn on Wilson Avenue next to the Holiday Inn. All three hotels did a good business; the proximity of the interstate highway as well as Forest Park and its many attractions helped fill the hotel rooms.

They walked through the lobby and took the elevator up to the third floor. Charlie and Jenny brought the police officers on plainclothes duty up-to-date on the events of that evening.

"I'm glad that you are okay, Charlie," Sergeant Mitch Cooper told him. Mitch had just arrived a few minutes earlier and was going to share the overnight guard duty with Jenny and Charlie.

"Thanks, Mitch. It was a close call."

"Hopefully the remainder of the night will be quiet."

"Let's hope so," Charlie agreed. "We only need to get to morning. The cavalry is on the way and will be here in the morning."

The three police officers who had been on duty for the past eight hours departed. Charlie and Mitch settled into the room with Dennis Sandhaven, while Jenny went into Fatima Cedar's room.

Fatima looked up from her laptop computer upon which she was intently working. "Hi, Jenny."

"Hi, Fatima. I'm glad to see that you are hard at work on that Intelligent Agency program. Some top computer experts from the federal government are on their way to St. Louis at this very moment. In the morning, they want to meet with you and Dennis in this hotel's conference room. The government wants to bring Intelligent Agency online tomorrow."

"You're kidding!"

"No, really. The program is ready, isn't it?"

"Yes, but everything is happening so swiftly!"

"More has happened than you know about." Jenny proceeded to give Fatima a detailed description of everything that had happened that evening.

Fatima listened with rapt attention. She was shocked to hear about the murder of the FBI official and about Charlie's rooftop battle with Sam Troutman.

"Charlie is a hero!" Fatima declared.

"Yes, he is," Jenny agreed.

"Jenny, you must marry this man. I will allow no dissent."

"Well, then I guess that settles it," Jenny laughed. "In the morning, I will inform Charlie of your proclamation about us."

"Good."

"You'll be pleased to know that a number of other persons share your opinion about Charlie and me."

"It is not just an opinion. It is the way things must be."

"I don't disagree," Jenny said. "He is my partner, my best friend, and my hero: I guess that I might as well make him my husband also."

Fatima smiled and nodded sagely.

In the adjacent room, Charlie recounted the same tale for Dennis Sandhaven and Mitch. Charlie, though, humbly downplayed his own role in the evening's events. Just as Charlie completed his narrative, his cell phone rang.

"Hi, Charlie," David said. "I'm coming up in the elevator now. I'll be at the door in less than a minute. I didn't want to startle you by just knocking on the door."

"Good idea." Charlie walked over, unlatched the door, and waited for David's arrival.

After admitting David to the room, he locked the door and latched it again. Charlie introduced David to Mitch, and the two men shook hands.

"Charlie has been telling us about his gun battle with your former partner," Mitch told David. "I can tell that Charlie is being too modest."

"Charlie is a modest man," David said. "He probably saved us all."

The men conversed for several more minutes. Then Dennis set up his laptop computer on the desk and logged onto the Intelligent Agency program. He wanted to make some last-minute preparations for the early morning arrival of the computer experts.

David stood up. "I'm going to go buy us some sodas and snacks. I'll buy some for Jenny and Fatima, too. Do you want me to stay on guard over there?"

"That will be fine," Charlie said. "Mitch and I will hold down the fort in here. I'm going to stay up all night. I might come over there in a couple of hours and trade rooms with you."

David grinned. "I'll bet that you will. You don't want to be away from Jenny very long."

Charlie laughed and rolled his eyes.

David went out of the room and walked about twenty feet down the hallway toward the alcove containing vending machines. A woman was standing in the alcove, scanning the various types of candy available in the snack machine. David assumed that she was a hotel guest staying in one of the other rooms on that floor.

"There are too many good choices," David said as he approached her. "I always have a hard time deciding what to buy."

"You won't need to make any decisions tonight," the woman said as she turned to face him.

To David's horror, she was holding a pistol equipped with a silencer. She fired three times. The first shot hit him in the chest, the second in the stomach, and the third bullet missed and hit the wall.

As he collapsed onto the hallway carpet, Maulana Hafsa hurried forward, hoping that the door to David's room was still open. Seeing that the door had closed, Maulana cursed quietly. Then she remembered that David probably had a key card in his pocket.

She turned and walked back toward his body. If he does not have a key, he must have been planning to knock on the door so that the cop could let him back into the room.

Maulana had surprised David, and now she was herself in for a surprise. In spite of being wounded, he managed to draw his gun from his shoulder holster while Maulana was looking toward the room door. Now, after she took two steps back toward him, he fired one shot that pierced her thigh.

His gun was not silenced, so the sound of the gunshot reverberated through much of the hotel. Maulana collapsed in pain on the floor just a few feet from where David lay.

Charlie came bolting out of the room, his gun drawn as he looked wildly in both directions for other attackers. He rushed forward, picked up the gun that Maulana had dropped, and bent down to examine David.

Two seconds later, Jenny came rushing out of her room. She held her pistol in one hand and her cell phone in the other hand.

"What happened?" she asked excitedly.

David groaned. "She ambushed me. She was pretending to buy candy."

"I don't see any blood on you," Charlie said. "Where are you hit?"

"Thank God for body armor," David said, placing his hands gingerly on his shirt beneath which was the bulletproof vest. "I think that I have some broken ribs, but the vest stopped the bullets."

Jenny went over to Maulana, who was holding her wounded leg and moaning. "You'll be all right," Jenny told the woman. "I'm going to call an ambulance."

Jenny dialed 911 on her cell phone, waited for a few seconds, looked at the screen, then dialed again. "Charlie, I can't get a signal."

"Perhaps your phone's battery needs recharging," Charlie suggested as he pulled out his own phone.

"No, it should be fine. I charged the battery this afternoon."

Charlie tried calling 911 from his own phone. "I can't get a signal either. This is weird. We are in the middle of the city."

"Perhaps the hotel's walls are interfering with the signal," Jenny suggested.

Mitch was watching the doorway of Charlie's room. "I will try calling from the room phone."

Several hotel guests down the hallway were looking out the doors of their rooms. One man stepped into the hallway.

"Was that a gunshot?" the man called to them. "What's happening?"

"There has been a shooting," Charlie said. "We are the police. Go back into your rooms and stay there until we tell you that it is safe to come out."

"Oh!" The man went back inside, and the other room doors closed.

"I doubt that this woman is here by herself," Jenny said. "There could be a hit team coming in behind her."

"Who is with you?" Charlie asked.

In spite of her pain, Maulana managed a cackling laugh. "I am the anvil upon which the hammer is descending."

"What does that mean?"

"You'll know the hammer when you see it," she continued to rave. "Actually, you probably won't see it. You will just die. You have already seen it, but you don't know that you have."

"She is delirious," Jenny suggested.

"I don't think so, but I know that we don't have time for riddles. I think that a hit team is coming in."

"I agree." Jenny's eyes continually probed up and down the hallway.

David rose up to one knee, grimacing with pain from the broken ribs. "I can help." He checked his gun.

Mitch reappeared in the doorway. "The hotel phone is not working either. I can't even get a dial tone. "

Fatima stood in the doorway of the room. "That woman is Maulana Hafsa. She is one of the radicals who works at Sandhaven Software. Every day Maulana had something negative to say about me. Every day she would sit at the lunch table spouting jihadist propaganda to the other radicals. She is their little lion."

Maulana snarled contemptuously. "Our little traitor appears. The hammer is also descending on you tonight, Fatima."

"How are they jamming both the cell phones and the land lines?" Charlie asked Maulana.

"Why should I tell you?"

"Primarily because you are likely to bleed to death unless we can call an ambulance to take you to a hospital."

"Drive me there yourself if you are so worried about me."

"I'm fairly certain that there is an ambush awaiting us on the parking lot," Charlie said. "If we step out of this hotel, we will be shot."

"Stay or leave, it does not matter," Maulana told him. "You will die either way."

"Charlie, we are too vulnerable in this hallway," Jenny said. "Let's get back into the rooms until we figure out what to do."

"Okay. First, though I want to check the elevators." With his gun held ready to fire, Charlie move cautiously down the hallway and approached the elevators.

Then, suddenly, all the lights went off and the hallway was engulfed in almost complete darkness.

"They might be coming now!" Charlie exclaimed. He half-expected armed figures equipped with night-vision goggles to appear at any moment.

"We'd better get back into the rooms," David said.

"What are we going to do about her?" Charlie asked.

"In spite of what she has done, I don't feel right about leaving her in the hallway," Jenny said.

"I have some medical training," Fatima volunteered. "We can bind her wound with a bed sheet to help stop the bleeding."

"Good," Jenny said. "Help me to get her into the room, Fatima."

"The hammer has begun its descent," Maulana snarled.

"It's good to see that you are not ungrateful," Jenny said sarcastically.

The bright screens of their cell phones provided a small amount of illumination as Jenny and Fatima supported Maulana as she hopped into the room on her good leg.

Charlie helped David back into their room. While Charlie locked and bolted the door, Mitch pulled open the drapes and the room was partially illuminated by the street lights as well as the lights from nearby businesses.

"This should help a little," Mitch said.

"Close those drapes, Mitch!" Charlie declared, realizing the danger.

At that moment, there was a pinging sound as the bullet punctured the glass balcony door. Mitch lurched backward and then collapsed dead onto the carpet. The bullet had penetrated his forehead.

"Get down!" Charlie commanded Dennis, who promptly complied.

The two men crouched behind a bed, startled by what had just happened.

"Jenny!" Charlie shouted. "Mitch was just killed by a sniper! Stay away from the windows! Take cover!"

"Okay!" Jenny called back. "We're down behind the beds! We are all right."

Two more shots smashed into the wall of Charlie's room, but neither shot came close to either man. Based upon the angle of the shots, Charlie tried to determine from where the sniper was shooting.

"I think that he might be firing from the parking lot," Charlie said in a very loud voice so that Jenny and Fatima could hear in the other room.

"He does not seem to have a good angle on this room," Dennis observed. "As long as we stay in this half of the room, I doubt that he can hit us."

"I agree," Charlie said. "However, he might be able to move somewhere that will give him a better angle, so we'd better stay down."

At that moment, someone in the hallway fired a torrent of bullets into the door of Charlie's room. Startled, Charlie drew his gun and fired back, uncertain whether the bullets would penetrate the fairly-heavy hotel room door.

"We have nowhere to take cover!" Dennis shouted. "We can't go forward, and we can't go back!"

Shaukat Khan, standing in the hallway, aimed his Uzi submachine gun at the door handle and blasted the lock away. The door began to swing open, and Shaukat took a cautious step forward. Although he had superior firepower, he knew that the police officers were armed.

While he squeezed the trigger of the Uzi, he kicked the door open, spraying the room with automatic weapon fire.

Then, suddenly, Shaukat heard running footsteps approaching him from behind. He quickly turned to confront the person, but Shaukat was not fast enough. With panther-like speed, Marcus closed in on his prey.

Marcus slammed into Shaukat, grabbing his head, and breaking his neck. As Shaukat collapsed dead onto the carpet, Marcus pulled the Uzi from his hand.

"Valentine! Halloran! Hold your fire! It's Marcus Augustine! I got him! You're safe for the moment."

Charlie, who had barely avoided Shaukat's final assault, had seen Marcus kill their attacker. Dennis and Charlie stood up and went forward toward the hallway.

"Jenny, it's okay!" Charlie called to his partner. "Bring Fatima back into the hallway." Charlie turned back toward Marcus. "There is a sniper down in the parking lot. He killed Mitch, the police officer who was with us here."

"You don't need to worry about that sniper," Marcus said. "Just after I parked my car, I saw him on the lot close to the highway. He was firing up at this room. I jumped out of my car and killed him with a headshot from my pistol." Marcus pulled out the expensive handgun, which was equipped with a silencer. "I'm sorry that I wasn't able to get him before he killed your police officer."

Marcus handed a wallet to Charlie. "I knew that you would want his identification, so I took this wallet of the pocket of his pants."

Charlie examined the contents of the wallet. "His name was Sharif Saffa. I'll be interested in finding out his background."

David came forward and looked intently at Marcus. "Who is this man?"

Charlie made the hurried introductions. "David, this is Marcus Augustine. He is the local private detective who rescued Fatima. Marcus, this is David Hummel, the FBI agent who was Sam Troutman's partner."

"You're lucky to still be alive," Marcus said.

"You've got that right," David agreed.

Charlie handed David the wallet. "When we are able to reestablish communication, you can give this information to the FBI and Homeland Security."

While the men spoke, Jenny was keeping a careful watch on the hallway. She glanced over at Marcus. "Can we leave the hotel now?"

"No. Sharif Saffa was covering the side door and north side parking lot to the hotel, but someone else must be covering the front entrance and front parking lot. They might still have two or three operatives out there."

"The cell phone signal is still being jammed," Jenny said.

"I'm going to slip out the side door and see if I can spot their operatives that are still active," Marcus said. "It's possible that another assault is going to be launched against this room, so you'd better get ready. All of you should lock yourself into this other room whose door is still intact."

"I have never met a private detective like you," David said. "You must have been in the military."

"Yes." Marcus smiled. "I was with special forces in Afghanistan. I primarily functioned as a sniper."

"Well, I'm certainly glad that we have your help tonight."

CHAPTER 17

▼

FINAL JEOPARDY

Hampton Avenue was normally a very busy street, but it was after midnight, so the traffic was fairly light.

After going out of a side door of the Holiday Inn, Marcus dashed behind a liquor store, then ran north across the entrance ramp to the highway.

He climbed up the embankment, stopping in a flower bed that had been planted along the side of the highway.

Apparently Saud Tariq did not see me or I would be a dead man now, Marcus reasoned. He looked up at the Drury Inn, attempting to find his opponent. Marcus's eyes scanned the balconies, but he could not see Saud Tariq anywhere.

Perhaps he has run around to the side of the Holiday Inn and is looking at balconies for me, Marcus thought with a grin.

Marcus understood his opponent well enough to know that his opponent had not run away in fear. Like me, he is a proud man, and a man who enjoys the challenge of having a worthy opponent.

Marcus removed his rifle from its case, rested it on his shoulder, and looked through the telescopic scope. He searched the windows of the Drury Inn, looking for gaps in curtains from which Tariq might be watching and perhaps taking aim upon him.

I wish that I had a night-vision scope on this rifle, he reflected. Night vision often came in handy during my days as a military sniper.

Then, suddenly, the moon came sailing out from behind some clouds, and the illumination improved.

As he focused in on the balconies, he spotted Saud Tariq on a balcony on the top floor of the hotel. The man was perfectly silhouetted against the moon. Looking through the telescopic scope of his own rifle, Tariq was scanning the roof and windows of the Holiday Inn.

Marcus felt a rush of adrenalin as he took careful aim at the silhouetted figure. Then, suddenly, as if guided by some survival instinct or sixth sense, Tariq looked sharply left, toward the highway. His eyes immediately found Marcus. Tariq started to take aim at his enemy, but he was much too late.

Marcus squeezed the trigger and fired.

Seconds later, Marcus watched the tall man topple forward over the railing. Tariq's body somersaulted as it fell toward the parking lot below; it reminded Marcus of an Olympic diver jumping off the high dive. Even at the moment of death, the man was graceful.

After Saud Tariq hit the pavement, Marcus hurried down the embankment and rushed across Hampton Avenue. He knew that a crowd would soon gather near the body, and the police and the television cameras and reporters would soon be there.

Marcus slipped back into the Holiday Inn. Moments after he entered the building, power was restored and the lights came back on. He took the elevator upstairs and went down the hallway.

Having heard the elevator doors open, Jenny and Charlie were on high alert as they peered out of the vending machine alcove where they were guarding Fatima and Dennis.

"Don't worry," Marcus called to them. "It's just me. I got the sniper. His body is on the parking lot of the Drury Inn. I'm fairly sure that he was the last of them."

"Good." Charlie holstered his gun as everyone breathed sighs of relief.

They took the elevator down to the lobby, walked across the parking lot, and across Hampton Avenue.

"We're police! Please move away from the body!" Charlie ordered as he and Jenny held up their badges.

About twenty persons had congregated on the Drury Inn parking lot near where the sniper had fallen. The wail of numerous police sirens gradually was becoming louder.

"It's Sam Troutman," David said as he approached the body of his former partner. He stood in silence for several seconds looking down at the man with two names: Sam Troutman and Saud Tariq.

"Well, his opening gambit was quite good, but his endgame needed work," David stated, concluding his period of reflection.

"That does seem to summarize things," Charlie said in agreement.

The next day, in the hotel's conference room, Fatima and Dennis would join forces with the visiting government officials and establish the Internet links that would activate the Intelligent Agency program on dozens of mainframe computers all over the country, giving the United States an invincible defense against biological warfare attacks. Any doomsday virus could easily be defeated by Intelligent Agency.

With backup upon backup, the Intelligent Agency program was now indestructible, and the persons who helped to create it finally felt safe.

Marcus and Fatima both received pleasant surprises. Dennis hired Marcus as the security chief for Sandhaven Software, and Dennis promoted Fatima to the position of director of programming and vice-president of the company.

However, before that day's final dramatic events, everyone did manage to get a few hours sleep as the waning moon completed its nightly trek through the sky.

Marcus had dreams of restoration, renewal, and resurrection in which he and his family walked in peaceful bliss in an eternal paradise.

With perfect clarity, Marcus saw a golden path before him. He had successfully sailed along the river of time toward this destination that he had so ardently desired to reach: love had indeed led him home.

Jenny dreamt of sitting by a campfire as she looked at the fire's reflection in the diamond of her engagement ring. Then, her glance moved up from the ring as she saw a cowboy walking over the hill on the horizon.

Charlie, in his own dream, walked through a desert at night. From a hilltop, he saw a beautiful maiden dressed in blue, illuminated by a fire burning bright, silhouetted by the glowing moon.

A great and wondrous sign appeared in heaven: a woman clothed with the sun, with the moon under her feet and a crown of twelve stars on her head.

Revelation 12:1

The Further Adventures of Charlie Valentine and Jenny Halloran

You can read two additional stories featuring Charlie Valentine and Jenny Halloran that are posted on the author's website at **JoeRogers.homestead.com**

These two mystery stories are **Murder in the Courthouse** and **The Case of the Missing Professor**. Both stories are free.

This website also has other mysteries, plays, family photos, and excerpts from some suspense novels.